Henry W. Lon

Poems of P

Oceanica. Australasia, Polynesia, and Miscellaneous Seas and Islands

Henry W. Longfellow

Poems of Places
Oceanica. Australasia, Polynesia, and Miscellaneous Seas and Islands

ISBN/EAN: 9783337845995

Printed in Europe, USA, Canada, Australia, Japan

Cover: Foto ©Andreas Hilbeck / pixelio.de

More available books at **www.hansebooks.com**

POEMS OF PLACES

EDITED BY

HENRY W. LONGFELLOW

It is the Soul that sees; the outward eyes
Present the object, but the Mind descries.
CRABBE.

OCEANICA.

AUSTRALASIA, POLYNESIA, AND MISCELLANEOUS
SEAS AND ISLANDS

BOSTON:
HOUGHTON, OSGOOD AND COMPANY.
The Riverside Press, Cambridge.
1879.

UNIVERSITY PRESS : WELCH, BIGELOW, & CO.,
CAMBRIDGE.

CONTENTS.

OCEANICA.

AUSTRALASIA.

MISCELLANEOUS.

APPENDIX.

EPILOGUE.

OCEANICA.

AUSTRALASIA.

INTRODUCTORY.

AUSTRALASIA.

THE sun is high in heaven; a favoring breeze
Fills the white sail and sweeps the rippling seas,
And the tall vessel walks her destined way,
And rocks and glitters in the curling spray.
Among the shrouds, all happiness and hope,
The busy seaman coils the rattling rope,
And tells his jest, and carols out his song,
And laughs his laughter, vehement and long;
Or pauses on the deck, to dream awhile
Of his babes' prattle and their mother's smile,
And nods the head, and waves the welcome hand,
To those who weep upon the lessening strand.
  His is the roving step and humor dry,
His the light laugh, and his the jocund eye;

And his the feeling which, in guilt or grief,
Makes the sin venial, and the sorrow brief.
But there are hearts, that merry deck below,
Of darker error, and of deeper woe, —
Children of wrath and wretchedness who grieve
Not for the country, but the crimes they leave,
Who, while for them on many a sleepless bed
The prayer is murmured and the tear is shed,
In exile and in misery, lock within
Their dread despair, their unrepented sin,
And in their madness dare to gaze on heaven,
Sullen and cold, unawed and unforgiven!

There the gaunt robber, stern in sin and shame,
Shows his dull features and his iron frame;
And tenderer pilferers creep in silence by,
With quivering lip, flushed brow, and vacant eye.
And some there are who, in their close of day,
With dropping jaw, weak step, and temples gray,
Go tottering forth, to find, across the wave,
A short sad sojourn, and a foreign grave;
And some, who look their long and last adieu
To the white cliffs that vanish from the view,
While youth still blooms, and vigor nerves the arm,
The blood flows freely, and the pulse beats warm.
The hapless female stands in silence there,
So weak, so wan, and yet so sadly fair,
That those who gaze, a rude untutored tribe,
Check the coarse question and the wounding gibe,
And look, and long to strike the fetter off,
And stay to pity, though they came to scoff.
Then o'er her cheek there runs a burning blush,

And the hot tears of shame begin to rush
Forth from their swelling orbs;—she turns away,
And her white fingers o'er her eyelids stray,
And still the tears through those white fingers glide,
Which strive to check them, or at least to hide!
And there the stripling, led to plunder's school,
Ere Passion slept, or Reason learned to rule,
Clasps his young hands, and beats his throbbing brain,
And looks with marvel on his galling chain.
O, you may guess, from that unconscious gaze,
His soul hath dreamed of those far-fading days,
When, rudely nurtured on the mountain's brow,
He tended day by day his father's plough;
Blest in his day of toil, his night of ease,
His life of purity, his soul of peace.
O, yes! to-day his soul hath backward been
To many a tender face and beauteous scene,—
The verdant valley and the dark brown hill,
The small fair garden, and its tinkling rill,
His grandame's tale, believed at twilight hour,
His sister singing in her myrtle bower,
And she, the maid, of every hope bereft,
So fondly loved, alas! so falsely left,—
The winding path, the dwelling in the grove,
The look of welcome, and the kiss of love,—
These are his dreams; but these are dreams of bliss!
Why do they blend with such a lot as his?
   And is there naught for him but grief and gloom,
A lone existence, and an early tomb?
Is there no hope of comfort and of rest
To the seared conscience and the troubled breast?

Oh, say not so! In some far distant clime,
Where lives no witness of his early crime,
Benignant Penitence may haply muse
On purer pleasures and on brighter views,
And slumbering Virtue wake at last to claim
Another being, and a fairer fame.

  Beautiful land! within whose quiet shore
Lost spirits may forget the stain they bore;
Beautiful land! with all thy blended shades
Of waste and wood, rude rocks, and level glades,
On thee, on thee I gaze, as Moslems look
To the blest islands of their Prophet's Book:
And oft I deem that, linked by magic spell,
Pardon and Peace upon thy valleys dwell,
Like two sweet Houris beckoning o'er the deep
The souls that tremble and the eyes that weep!
Therefore on thee undying sunbeams throw
Their clearest radiance and their warmest glow,
And tranquil nights, cool gales, and gentle showers
Make bloom eternal in thy sinless bowers.
Green is thy turf; stern Winter doth not dare
To breathe his blast, and leave a ruin there,
And the charmed ocean roams thy rocks around,
With softer motion and with sweeter sound:
Among thy blooming flowers and-blushing fruit
The whispering of young birds is never mute,
And never doth the streamlet cease to well
Through its old channel in the hidden dell.
O, if the Muse of Greece had ever strayed,
In solemn twilight, through thy forest shade,
And swept her lyre, and waked thy meads along

The liquid echo of her ancient song,
Her fabling Fancy in that hour had found
Voices of music, shapes of grace, around;
Among thy trees, with merry step and glance,
The Dryad then had wound her wayward dance,
And the cold Naiad in thy waters fair
Bathed her white breast, and wrung her dripping hair.

Beautiful land! upon so pure a plain
Shall Superstition hold her hated reign?
Must Bigotry build up her cheerless shrine
In such an air, on such an earth as thine?
Alas! Religion from thy placid isles
Veils the warm splendor of her heavenly smiles,
And the wrapt gazer in the beauteous plan
Sees nothing dark — except the soul of Man.

Sweet are the links that bind us to our kind,
Meek, but unyielding, — felt, but undefined;
Sweet is the love of brethren, sweet the joy
Of a young mother in her cradled boy,
And sweet is childhood's deep and earnest glow
Of reverence for a father's head of snow!
Sweeter than all, ere our young hopes depart,
The quickening throb of an impassioned heart,
Beating in silence, eloquently still,
For one loved soul that answers to its thrill.
But where thy smile, Religion, hath not shone,
The chain is riven, and the charm is gone;
And, unawakened by thy wondrous spell,
The Feelings slumber in their silent cell.

Hushed is the voice of labor and of mirth,
The light of day is sinking from the earth,

And Evening mantles in her dewy calm
The couch of one who cannot heed its balm.
Lo! where the chieftain on his matted bed
Leans the faint form, and hangs the feverish head!
There is no lustre in his wandering eye,
His forehead hath no show of majesty;
His gasping lip, too weak for wail or prayer,
Scarce stirs the breeze, and leaves no echo there;
And his strong arm, so nobly wont to rear
The feathered target or the ashen spear,
Drops powerless and cold! the pang of death
Locks the set teeth and chokes the struggling breath,
And the last glimmering of departing day
Lingers around to herald life away.

   Is there no duteous youth to sprinkle now
One drop of water on his lip and brow?
No dark-eyed maid to bring with soundless foot
The lulling potion or the healing root?
No tender look to meet his wandering gaze?
No tone of fondness, heard in happier days,
To soothe the terrors of the spirit's flight,
And speak of mercy and of hope to-night?

   All love, all leave him! — terrible and slow
Along the crowd the whispered murmurs grow.
"The hand of Heaven is on him! is it ours
To check the fleeting of his numbered hours?
Oh, not to us, — oh, not to us is given
To read the book, or thwart the will, of Heaven!
Away, away!" and each familiar face
Recoils in horror from his sad embrace;
The turf on which he lies is hallowed ground,

The sullen priest stalks gloomily around,
And shuddering friends, that dare not soothe or save,
Hear the last groan, and dig the destined grave.
The frantic widow folds upon her breast
Her glittering trinkets and her gorgeous vest,
Circles her neck with many a mystic charm,
Clasps the rich bracelet on her desperate arm,
Binds her black hair, and stains her eyelid's fringe
With the jet lustre of the henna's tinge;
Then, on the spot where those dear ashes lie,
In bigot transport sits her down to die.
Her swarthy brothers mark the wasted cheek,
The straining eyeball, and the stifled shriek,
And sing the praises of her deathless name,
As the last flutter racks her tortured frame.
They sleep together: o'er the natural tomb
The lichened pine rears up its form of gloom,
And lorn acacias shed their shadow gray,
Bloomless and leafless, o'er the buried clay.
And often there, when calmly, coldly bright,
The midnight moon flings down her ghastly light,
With solemn murmur and with silent tread,
The dance is ordered, and the verse is said,
And sights of wonder, sounds of spectral fear,
Scare the quick glance and chill the startled ear.

    Yet direr visions e'en than these remain;
A fiercer guiltiness, a fouler stain!
Oh, who shall sing the scene of savage strife,
Where Hatred glories in the waste of life?
The hurried march, the looks of grim delight,
The yell, the rush, the slaughter, and the flight,

The arms unwearied in the cruel toil,
The hoarded vengeance and the rifled spoil,
And, last of all, the revel in the wood,
The feast of death, the banqueting of blood,
When the wild warrior gazes on his foe
Convulsed beneath him in his painful throe,
And lifts the knife, and kneels him down to drain
The purple current from the quivering vein?
Cease, cease the tale; and let the ocean's roll
Shut the dark horror from my wildered soul!
    And are there none to succor? none to speed
A fairer feeling and a holier creed?
Alas! for this, upon the ocean blue,
Lamented Cook, thy pennon hither flew;
For this, undaunted, o'er the raging brine
The venturous Frank upheld his Saviour's sign.
Unhappy Chief! while Fancy thus surveys
The scattered islets and the sparkling bays,
Beneath whose cloudless sky and gorgeous sun
Thy life was ended, and thy voyage done,
In shadowy mist thy form appears to glide,
Haunting the grove, or floating on the tide;
Oh, there was grief for thee, and bitter tears,
And racking doubts through long and joyless years;
And tender tongues that babbled of the theme,
And lonely hearts that doated on the dream.
Pale Memory deemed she saw thy cherished form
Snatched from the foe, or rescued from the storm;
And faithful Love, unfailing and untired,
Clung to each hope, and sighed as each expired.
On the bleak desert, or the tombless sea,

No prayer was said, no requiem sung for thee;
Affection knows not whether o'er thy grave
The ocean murmur or the willow wave;
But still the beacon of thy sacred name
Lights ardent souls to Virtue and to Fame,
Still Science mourns thee, and the grateful Muse
Wreathes the green cypress for her own Pérouse.

But not thy death shall mar the gracious plan,
Nor check the task thy pious toil began;
O'er the wide waters of the bounding main
The Book of Life must win its way again,
And, in the regions by thy fate endeared,
The cross be lifted, and the altar reared.

With furrowed brow and cheek serenely fair,
The calm wind wandering o'er his silver hair,
His arm uplifted, and his moistened eye
Fixed in deep rapture on the golden sky, —
Upon the shore, through many a billow driven,
He kneels at last, the Messenger of Heaven!
Long years, that rank the mighty with the weak,
Have dimmed the flush upon his faded cheek,
And many a dew and many a noxious damp,
The daily labor, and the nightly lamp,
Have reft away, forever reft, from him
The liquid accent and the buoyant limb.
Yet still within him aspirations swell
Which time corrupts not, sorrow cannot quell, —
The changeless zeal, which on, from land to land,
Speeds the faint foot and nerves the withered hand,
And the mild Charity, which, day by day,
Weeps every wound and every stain away,

Rears the young bud on every blighted stem,
And longs to comfort where she must condemn.
With these, through storms and bitterness and wrath,
In peace and power he holds his onward path,
Curbs the fierce soul, and sheathes the murderous steel,
And calms the passions he hath ceased to feel.

Yes! he hath triumphed! — while his lips relate
The sacred story of his Saviour's fate,
While to the search of that tumultuous horde
He opens wide the Everlasting Word,
And bids the soul drink deep of Wisdom there,
In fond devotion, and in fervent prayer,
In speechless awe the wonder-stricken throng
Check their rude feasting and their barbarous song:
Around his steps the gathering myriads crowd,
The chief, the slave, the timid, and the proud;
Of various features, and of various dress,
Like their own forest-leaves, confused and numberless.
Where shall your temples, where your worship be,
Gods of the air, and rulers of the sea?
In the glad dawning of a kinder light,
Your blind adorer quits your gloomy rite,
And kneels in gladness on his native plain,
A happier votary at a holier fane.

Beautiful land, farewell! — when toil and strife,
And all the sighs and all the sins of life
Shall come about me, — when the light of Truth
Shall scatter the bright mists that dazzled youth,
And Memory muse in sadness on the past,
And mourn for pleasures far too sweet to last;
How often shall I long for some green spot,

Where, not remembering, and remembered not,
With no false verse to deck my lying bust,
With no fond tear to vex my mouldering dust,
This busy brain may find its grassy shrine,
And sleep, untroubled, in a shade like thine!

William Mackworth Praed.

AUSTRALIA.

AUSTRALIA, in her varied forms, expands,
And opens to the sky her hundred lands,
From where the day-beam paints the waters blue,
Around the blessed islands of Arroo,
And life, in all its myriad mouldings, plays,
Amid the beauty of the tropic blaze, --
Where summer watches with undying eye,
And equal day and night divide the sky, -
Where the throned Phœbus wakens all the flowers,
To do him homage in his own bright bowers,
And Cynthia, on her empyrean height,
Holds crowded levee through the livelong night,
Where starlight is a gala of the skies,
And sunset is a cloud sketched paradise;
Away, away, to where the billows rave,
Around the quenched volcano's echoing cave,
Where she, the lonely beauty, sits and smiles,
In sweetness, like an orphan of the isles,
Fair as fair Aphrodite on the deep,
But lone as Ariadne on her steep!
Away,   away, to where the dolphins play,

And the sea-lion tracks his pathless way;
Away, — away, where southern icebergs roll,
Upon the troubled billows round the pole;
Where the bold mariner, whose course has run
Beyond the journey of the circling sun,
Condemned, for lingering months, to sleep and wake
By nights that cloud not, days that never break,
To watch by stars that fade not from the eye,
And moons that have no rival in the sky,
Lies down to slumber, and awakes to weep
For brighter scenes that rose upon his sleep,
And many a glance from faces far away,
That turned the darkness into more than day, —
Till his fond bosom glows with fancy's fires,
And hope embodies all the heart desires,
And every vision of his distant home
Warms, like a prophecy of days to come!

Isles of the Orient! gardens of the East!
Thou giant secret of the liquid waste,
Long ages in untrodden paths concealed,
Or, but in glimpses faint and few revealed,
Like some chimera of the ocean-caves,
Some dark and sphinx-like riddle of the waves,
Till he, the northern Œdipus, unfurled
His venturous sail, and solved it to the world!
Surpassing beauty sits upon thy brow,
But darkness veils thy all of time, save now;
Enshrouded in the shadows of the past,
And secret in thy birth as is the blast!
If, when the waters and the land were weighed,

Thy vast foundations in the deep were laid;
Or, mid the tempests of a thousand years,
Where through the depths her shell the mermaid steers,
Mysterious workmen wrought unseen at thee,
And reared thee, like a Babel, in the sea;
If Afric's dusky children sought the soil
Which yields her fruits without the tiller's toil;
Or, southward wandering on his dubious way,
Came to thy blooming shores the swarth Malay;—
'T is darkness all! long years have o'er thee rolled
Their flight unnoted, and their tale untold!
But beautiful thou art, as fancy deems
The visioned regions of her sweetest dreams;
Fair as the Moslem, in his fervor, paints
The promised valleys of his prophet's saints;
Bright with the brightness which the poet's eye
Flings o'er the long-lost bowers of Araby!
The soul of beauty haunts thy sunny glades,
The soul of music whispers through thy shades,
And Nature, gazing on her loveliest plan,
Sees all supremely excellent but man!

Now on my soul the rising vision warms,
But mingled in a thousand lovely forms.
Methinks I see Australian landscapes still,
But softer beauty sits on every hill;
I see bright meadows decked in livelier green,
The yellow cornfield, and the blossomed bean;
A hundred flocks o'er smiling pastures roam,
And hark! the music of the harvest-home.
Methinks I hear the hammer's busy sound,

And cheerful hum of human voices round, —
The laughter, and the song that lightens toil,
Sung in the language of my native isle;
In mighty bays unnumbered navies ride,
Or come and go upon the distant tide,
In land-locked harbors rest their giant forms,
Or boldly launch upon the "Bay of Storms";
While the swarth native crowns the glorious plan
In all the towering dignity of man.

The vision leads me on by many a stream;
And spreading cities crowd upon my dream,
Where turrets darkly frown, and lofty spires
Point to the stars, and sparkle in their fires.
Here Sydney gazes from the mountain-side,
Narcissus-like, upon the glassy tide!
There Hobart stretches, where the Derwent sees
Her flaxen ringlets tremble in the breeze!
O'er rising towns Notasian commerce reigns,
And temples crowd Tasmania's lovely plains,
And browsing goats, without a keeper, stray,
Where the bushranger tracked the covert way.

The prospect varies in an endless range,
Villas and lawns go by in ceaseless change.
Glenfinlas! thou hast hundred rival vales,
Where quiet hamlets deck the sloping dales;
And, wafted on the gale from many a dell,
Methinks I hear the village Sabbath bell!
And now the anthem swells; on every hand
A cloud of incense gathers o'er the land;

Faith upward mounts, upon devotion's wings,
And, like the lark, at heaven's high portal sings;
From myriad tongues the song of praise is poured,
And o'er them floats "the Spirit of the Lord."

Thomas Kibble Hervey.

DOWN IN AUSTRALIA.

QUAFF a cup, and send a cheer up for the Old Land !
    We have heard the Reapers shout,
    For the Harvest going out,
With the smoke of battle closing round the bold Land;
    And our message shall be hurled
    Up the ringing sides o' the world,
There are true hearts beating for you in the Gold Land.

We are with you in your battles, brave and bold Land !
    For the old ancestral tree
    Striketh root beneath the sea,
And it beareth fruit of Freedom in the Gold Land !
    We shall come too, if you call,
    We shall fight on if you fall,
Cromwell's land must never be a bought and sold land.

O, the standard of the Lord wave o'er the Old Land !
    For, the waiting world holds breath
    While she treads the dew of Death,
With the sleeve of Peace stript up from her bare, bold
    hand :
    And her ruddy Rose will bloom

On the bosom and the tomb
Of her many Heroes fallen for the Old Land.

O, a terror to the Tyrant is the Old Land!
    He remembers how she stood
    With her raiment rolled in blood,
When the tide of battle burst upon the bold Land,
    And he looks with darkened face,
    For he knows the hero-race
Sweep the harp of Freedom — draw her Sword with
    bold hand.

Let thy glorious voice be heard, thou great and bold
    Land!
    Speak the one victorious word,
    And fair Freedom's wandered Bird
Shall wing back with leaf of promise from the Old Land!
    And the peoples shall come out
    From their slavery, with a shout
For the new world greeting in the Future's Gold Land!

When the smoke of Battle rises from the Old Land,
    You shall see the Tyrant down,
    You shall see the ransomed crown;
On the brow of prisoned peoples, freed with bold hand!
    She shall thrash her foes like corn;
    They shall eat the bread of scorn;
And will sing her song of Triumph in the Gold Land.

Quaff a cup, and send a cheer up from the Gold Land!
    We have heard the Reapers shout,

For the Harvest going out,
Seen the smoke of battle closing round the bold Land!
And our message shall be hurled
Up the ringing sides o' the world,
There are true hearts down here, beating for the Old
Land.

Gerald Massey.

WESTERN AUSTRALIA.

O BEAUTEOUS Southland! land of yellow air,
   That hangeth o'er thee slumbering, and doth hold
The moveless foliage of thy valleys fair
   And wooded hills, like aureole of gold.

O thou, discovered ere the fitting time,
   Ere Nature in completion turned thee forth!
Ere aught was finished but thy peerless clime,
   Thy virgin breath allured the amorous North.

O land, God made thee wondrous to the eye!
   But his sweet singers thou hast never heard;
He left thee, meaning to come by and by,
   And give rich voice to every bright-winged bird.

He painted with fresh hues thy myriad flowers,
   But left them scentless: ah! their woful dole,
Like sad reproach of their Creator's powers,
   To make so sweet fair bodies, void of soul.

He gave thee trees of odorous precious wood,
   But midst them all bloomed not one tree of fruit;

He looked, but said not that his work was good,
    When leaving thee all perfumeless and mute.

He blessed thy flowers with honey: every bell
    Looks earthward, sunward, with a yearning wist;
But no bee-lover ever notes the swell
    Of hearts, like lips, a-hungering to be kist.

O strange land, thou art virgin! thou art more
    Than fig-tree barren! Would that I could paint
For others' eyes the glory of the shore
    Where last I saw thee; but the senses faint

In soft delicious dreaming when they drain
    Thy wine of color. Virgin fair thou art,
All sweetly fertile, waiting with soft pain
    The spouse who comes to wake thy sleeping heart.

                              John Boyle O'Reilly.

WIDDERIN'S RACE.

A HORSE amongst ten thousand! on the verge,
    The extremest verge, of equine life he stands;
Yet mark his action, as those wild young colts
Freed from the stock-yard gallop whinnying up;
See how he trots towards them, — nose in air,
Tail arched, and his still sinewy legs out-thrown
In gallant grace before him! A brave beast
As ever spurned the moorland, ay, and more, —
He bore me once, — such words but smite the truth
I' the outer ring, while vivid memory wakes,

Recalling now, the passion and the pain,—
He bore me once from earthly Hell to Heaven!

The sight of fine old Widderin (that's his name,
Caught from a peak, the topmost rugged peak
Of tall Mount Widderin, towering to the North
Most like a steed's head, with full nostrils blown,
And ears pricked up),—the sight of Widderin brings
That day of days before me, whose strange hours
Of fear and anguish, ere the sunset, changed
To hours of such content and full-veined joy
As Heaven can give our mortal lives but once.

Well, here's the story: While yon bush-fires sweep
The distant ranges, and the river's voice
Pipes a thin treble through the heart of drouth,
While the red heaven like some huge caldron's top
Seems with the heat a-simmering, better far
In place of riding tilt 'gainst such a sun,
Here in the safe veranda's flowery gloom,
To play the dwarfish Homer to a song,
Whereof myself am hero:

                              Two decades
Have passed since that wild autumn-time when last
The convict hordes from near Van Diemen, freed
By force or fraud, swept, like a blood-red fire,
Inland from beach to mountain, bent on raid
And rapine.

      *   *   *

So, in late autumn,—'t was a marvellous morn,
With breezes from the calm snow-river borne

That touched the air, and stirred it into thrills,
Mysterious and mesmeric, a bright mist
Lapping the landscape like a golden trance,
Swathing the hill-tops with fantastic veils,
And o'er the moorland-ocean quivering light
As gossamer threads drawn down the forest aisles
At dewy dawning, — on this marvellous morn,
I, with four comrades, in this selfsame spot,
Watched the fair scene, and drank the spicy airs,
That held a subtiler spirit than our wine,
And talked and laughed, and mused in idleness, —
Weaving vague fancies, as our pipe-wreaths curled
Fantastic in the sunlight! I, with head
Thrown back, and cushioned snugly, and with eyes
Intent on one grotesque and curious cloud,
Puffed upward, that now seemed to take the shape
Of a Dutch tulip, now a Turk's face topped
By folds on folds of turban limitless, —
Heard suddenly, just as the clock chimed one,
To melt in musical echoes up the hills,
Quick footsteps on the gravelled path without, —
Steps of the couriers of calamity, —
So my heart told me, — ere with blanched regards,
Two stalwart herdsmen on our threshold paused,
Panting, with lips that writhed, and awful eyes ; —
A breath's space in each other's eyes we glared,
Then, swift as interchange of lightning thrusts
In deadly combat, question and reply
Clashed sharply, "What! the Rangers?" "Ay, by
     Heaven!
And loosed in force, — the hell-hounds!" "Whither
     bound?"

I stammered, hoarsely. "Bound," the elder said,
"Southward!—four stations had they sacked and burnt,
And now, drunk, furious — " But I stopped to hear
No more: with booming thunder in mine ears,
And blood-flushed eyes, I rushed to Widderin's side,
Drew tight the girths, upgathered curb and rein,
And sprang to horse ere yet our laggard friends —
Now trooping from the green veranda's shade —
Could dream of action!

               Love had winged my will,
For to the southward fair Garoopna held
My all of hope, life, passion; she whose hair
(Its tiniest strand of waving, witch-like gold)
Had caught my heart, entwined, and bound it fast,
As 't were some sweet enchautment's heavenly net!

I only gave a hand-wave in farewell,
Shot by, and o'er the endless moorland swept
(Endless it seemed, as those weird, measureless plains,
Which, in some nightmare vision, stretch and stretch
Towards infinity!) like some lone ship
O'er wastes of sailless waters: now, a pine,
The beacon pine gigantic, whose grim crown
Signals the far land-mariner from out
Gaunt boulders of the gray-backed Organ hill,
Rose on my sight, a mist-like, wavering orb,
The while, still onward, onward, onward still,
With motion winged, elastic, equable,
Brave Widderin cleaved the air-tides, tossed aside
The winds as waves, their swift, invisible breasts

Hissing with foam-like noise when pressed and pierced
By that keen head and fiery-crested form!

The lonely shepherd guardian on the plains,
Watching his sheep through languid, half-shut eyes,
Looked up, and marvelled, as we passed him by,
Thinking, perchance, it was a glorious thing,
So dressed, so booted, so caparisoned,
To ride such bright blood-coursers unto death!
Two sun-blacked natives, slumbering in the grass,
Just rose betimes to 'scape the trampling hoofs,
And hurled hot curses at me as I sped;
While here and there the timid kangaroo
Blundered athwart the mole-hills, and in puffs
Of steamy dust-cloud vanished like a mote!

Onward, still onward, onward, onward still!
And lo! thank Heaven, the mighty Organ hill,
That seemed a dim blue cloudlet at the start,
Hangs in aerial, fluted cliffs aloft, —
And still as through the long, low glacis borne,
Beneath the gorge borne ever at wild speed,
I saw the mateless mountain eagle wheel
Beyond the stark height's topmost pinnacle;
I heard his shriek of rage and ravin die
Deep down the desolate dells, as far behind
I left the gorge, and far before me swept
Another plain, tree-bordered now, and bound
By the clear river gurgling o'er its bed.

By this, my panting, but unconquered steed
Had thrown his small head backward, and his breath

Through the red nostrils burst in labored sighs;
I bent above his outstretched neck, I threw
My quivering arms about him, murmuring low,
"Good horse! brave heart! a little longer bear
The strain, the travail; and thenceforth for thee
Free pastures all thy days, till death shall come!
Ah, many and many a time, my noble bay,
Her lily hand hath wandered through thy mane,
Patted thy rainbow neck, and brought thee ears
Of daintiest corn from out the farmhouse loft,—
Help, help to save her now!"

                        I'll vow the brute
Heard me, and comprehended what he heard!
He shook his proud crest madly, and his eye
Turned for a moment sideways, flashed in mine
A lightning gleam, whose fiery language said,
"I know my lineage, will not shame my sire,—
My sire, who rushed triumphant 'twixt the flags,
And frenzied thousands, when on Epsom downs
Arcturus won the Derby! no, nor shame
My granddam, whose clean body, half enwrought
Of air, half fire, through swirls of desert sand
Bore Sheik Abdallah headlong on his prey!"

At last came forest shadows, and the road
Winding through bush and bracken, and at last
The hoarse stream rumbling o'er its quartz-sown crags.

"No, no! stanch Widderin! pause not now to drink;
An hour hence, and thy dainty nose shall dip

In richest wine, poured jubilantly forth
To quench thy thirst, my Beauty! but press on,
Nor heed these sparkling waters." God! my brain's
On fire once more! an instant tells me all;
All! life or death, — salvation or despair!
For yonder, o'er the wild grass-matted slope
The house stands, or it stood but yesterday.

A Titan cry of inarticulate joy
I raised, as, calm and peaceful in the sun,
Shone the fair cottage, and the garden-close,
Wherein, white-robed, unconscious, sat my Love
Lilting a low song to the birds and flowers.
She heard the hoof-strokes, saw me, started up,
And with her blue eyes wider than their wont,
And rosy lips half tremulous, rushed to meet
And greet me swiftly. "Up, dear Love!" I cried,
"The Convicts, the Bush-rangers! let us fly!"
Ah, then and there you should have seen her, friend,
My noble, beauteous Helen! not a tear,
Nor sob, and scarce a transient pulse-quiver,
As, clasping hand in hand, her fairy foot
Lit like a small bird on my horseman's boot,
And up into the saddle, lithe and light,
Vaulting she perched, her bright curls round my face!

We crossed the river, and, dismounting, led
O'er the steep slope of blended rock and turf
The wearied horse, and there behind a Tor
Of castellated bluestone, paused to sweep
With young keen eyes the broad plain stretched afar,

Serene and autumn-tinted at our feet :
" Either," said I, " these devils have gone east,
To meet with bloodhound Desborough in his rage
Between the granite passes of Luxorme,
Or else — dear Christ ! my Helen, low ! stoop low ! "
(These words were hissed in horror, for just then,
'Twixt the deep hollows of the river-vale,
The miscreants, with mixed shouts and curses, poured
Down through the flinty gorge tumultuously,
Seeming, we thought, in one fierce throng to charge
Our hiding-place.) I seized my Widderin's head,
Blindfolding him, for with a single neigh
Our fate were sealed o' the instant! As they rode,
Those wild, foul-languaged demons by our lair,
Scarce twelve yards off, my troubled steed shook wide
His streaming mane, stamped on the earth, and pawed
So loudly, that the sweat of agony rolled
Down my cold forehead; at which point I felt
My arm clutched, and a voice I did not know
Dropped the low murmur from pale, shuddering lips,
" O God ! if in those brutal hands I fall,
Living, look not into your mother's face
Or any woman's more ! "

                              What time had passed
Above our bowed heads, we pent, pinioned there
By awe and nameless horror, who shall tell?
Minutes, perchance, by mortal measurement,
Eternity by heart-throbs !   when at length
We turned, and eyes of mutual wonder raised,
We gazed on alien faces, haggard, worn,

And strange of feature as the faces born
In fever and delirium! Were we saved?
We scarce could comprehend it, till from out
The neighboring oak-wood rode our friends at speed,
With clang of steel, and eyebrows bent in wrath.
But, warned betimes, the wily ruffians fled
Far up the forest-coverts, and beyond
The dazzling snow-line of the distant hills,
Their yells of fiendish laughter pealing faint
And fainter from the cloudland, and the mist
That closed about them like an ash-gray shroud:
Yet were these wretches marked for imminent death:
The next keen sunrise pierced the savage gorge,
To which we tracked them, where, mere beasts at bay,
Grimly they fought, and brute by brute they fell.

Paul Hamilton Hayne.

THE AUSTRALIAN SHEPHERD.

'T IS cold and rainy on this winter night,
  But one whom I have known is with his flocks
At noonday in the summer of the South.
Before the sun the colors of the spring
Fade from the forest, and the odorous air
Is heated through and through. He takes his seat
On other earth, surrounded by strange plants.
He slays the wild dog and the stinging snake.
He has a rifle by him in the grass,
Wherewith he hunts the leaping kangaroo.
His dogs keep watch beside him. There he sleeps, —
What lies between us? All this bulky globe,

A chest of secrets, with a heart of fire
And crust of fossils.
     When the summer night
Falls over that great island in the south
Whereon his flocks repose, the Polar Star,
Once never lost by ancient mariners
In their confined adventures on the sea,
Peers not above the horizon, — lost to him
Forever ; but the splendid Southern Cross,
And those two clouds which bear Magellan's name,
Two clouds of clustered stars in the clear sky,
Hang nightly, far above the winds that blow
Around our planet, changeless films of light.
And when Orion and the wandering moon
Come with familiar aspect, they remind
The exile of the land on which they shone
When he first saw them, and his earliest friends,
And hills and streams and meadows of his youth,
And this old gabled house where he was born.
       Philip Gilbert Hamerton.

A DEATH IN THE BUSH.

THE hut was built of bark and shrunken slabs
 That wore the marks of many rains, and showed
Dry flaws, wherein had crept and nestled rot.
Moreover, round the bases of the bark
Were left the tracks of flying forest fires,
As you may see them on the lower bole
Of every elder of the native woods.

For, ere the early settlers came and stocked
These wilds with sheep and kine, the grasses grew
So that they took the passing pilgrim in,
And whelmed him, like a running sea, from sight.

And therefore, through the fiercer summer months,
While all the swamps were rotten, while the flats
Were baked and broken; when the clayey rifts
Yawned wide, half choked with drifted herbage, past
Spontaneous flames would burst from thence, and race
Across the prairies all day long.

                              At night
The winds were up, and then with fourfold speed,
A harsh gigantic growth of smoke and fire
Would roar along the bottoms, in the wake
Of fainting flocks of parrots, wallaroos,
And wildered wild things, scattering right and left,
For safety vague, throughout the general gloom.

Anon, the nearer hillside growing trees
Would take the surges; thus, from bough to bough,
Was borne the flaming terror! Bole and spire,
Rank after rank, now pillared, ringed, and rolled
In blinding blaze, stood out against the dead
Down-smothered dark, for fifty leagues away.

For fifty leagues! and when the winds were strong,
For fifty more! But, in the olden time,
These fires were counted as the harbingers
Of life-essential storms; since out of smoke

And heat there came across the midnight ways
Abundant comfort, with upgathered clouds,
And runnels babbling of a plenteous fall.

So comes the Southern gale at evenfall
(The swift "brickfielder" of the local folk)
About the streets of Sydney, when the dust
Lies burnt on glaring windows, and the men
Look forth from doors of drouth, and drink the change
With thirsty haste and that most thankful cry
Of, "Here it is — the cool, bright, blessed rain!"

The hut, I say, was built of bark and slabs,
And stood, the centre of a clearing, hemmed
By hurdle-yards, and ancients of the blacks :
These moped about their lazy fires, and sang
Wild ditties of the old days, with a sound
Of sorrow, like an everlasting wind,
Which mingled with the echoes of the noon,
And moaned amongst the noises of the night.

From thence a cattle-track, with link to link,
Ran off against the fishpools, to the gap,
Which sets you face to face with gleaming miles
Of broad Orara, winding in amongst
Black, barren ridges, where the nether spurs
Are fenced about by cotton-scrub, and grass
Blue-bitten with the salt of many droughts.

'T was here the shepherd housed him every night,
And faced the prospect like a patient soul;

Borne up by some vague hope of better days,
And God's fine blessing in his faithful wife ;
Until the humor of his malady
Took cunning changes from the good to bad,
And laid him lastly on a bed of death.

Two months thereafter, when the summer heat
Had roused the serpent from his rotten lair,
And made a noise of locusts in the boughs,
It came to this, that, as the blood-red sun
Of one fierce day of many slanted down
Obliquely past the nether jags of peaks
And gulfs of mist, the tardy night came vexed
By belted clouds, and scuds that wheeled and whirled
To left and right about the brazen clifts
Of ridges, rigid with a leaden gloom.

Then took the cattle to the forest camps
With vacant terror, and the hustled sheep
Stood dumb against the hurdles, even like
A fallen patch of shadowed mountain snow ;
And ever through the curlew's call afar
The storm grew on, while round the stinted slabs
Sharp snaps and hisses came, and went, and came,
The huddled tokens of a mighty blast
Which ran with an exceeding bitter cry
Across the tumbled fragments of the hills,
And through the sluices of the gorge and glen.

So, therefore, all about the shepherd's hut
That space was mute, save when the fastened dog,
Without a kennel, caught a passing glimpse

Of firelight moving through the lighted chinks;
For then he knew the hints of warmth within,
And stood, and set his great pathetic eyes,
In wind and wet, imploring to be loosed.

Not often now the watcher left the couch
Of him she watched; since, in his fitful sleep,
His lips would stir to wayward themes, and close
With bodeful catches. Once she moved away,
Half deafened by terrific claps, and stooped,
And looked without, to see a pillar dim
Of gathered gusts and fiery rain.
                                        Anon,
The sick man woke, and, startled by the noise,
Stared round the room, with dull delirious sight,
At this wild thing and that; for, through his eyes,
The place took fearful shapes, and fever showed
Strange crosswise lights about his pillow-head.
He, catching there at some phantasmic help,
Sat upright on the bolster, with a cry
Of, "Where is Jesus? — it is bitter cold!"
And then, because the thundercalls outside
Were mixed for him with slanders of the past,
He called his weeping wife by name, and said,
"Come closer, darling! we shall speed away
Across the seas, and seek some mountain home,
Shut in from liars, and the wicked words
That track us day and night, and night and day."

So waned the sad refrain. And those poor lips,
Whose latest phrases were for peace, grew mute,
And into everlasting silence passed.

As fares a swimmer who hath lost his breath
In wildering seas afar from any help,
Who, fronting Death, can never realize
The dreadful presence, but is prone to clutch
At every weed upon the weltering wave;
So fared the watcher, poring o'er the last
Of him she loved, with dazed and stupid stare;
Half conscious of the sudden loss and lack
Of all that bound her life, but yet without
The power to take her mighty sorrow in.

Then came a patch or two of starry sky;
And through a reef of cloven thunder-cloud
The soft moon looked : a patient face beyond
The fierce impatient shadows of the slopes,
And the harsh voices of the broken hills !
A patient face, and one which came and wrought
A lovely silence like a silver mist
Across the rainy relics of the storm.

For in the breaks and pauses of her light
The gale died out in gusts; yet evermore
About the roof-tree, on the dripping eaves,
The damp wind loitered; and a fitful drift
Sloped through the silent curtains, and athwart
The dead.

          There, when the glare had dropped behind
A mighty ridge of gloom, the woman turned
And sat in darkness face to face with God,
And said — "I know," she said, "that Thou art wise;

That when we build and hope, and hope and build,
And see our best things fall, it comes to pass
Forevermore that we must turn to Thee!
And therefore now, because I cannot find
The faintest token of Divinity
In this my latest sorrow, let thy light
Inform mine eyes, so I may learn to look
On something past the sight which shuts, and blinds,
And seems to drive me wholly, Lord, from thee."

Now waned the moon beyond complaining depths;
And, as the dawn looked forth from showery woods
(Whereon had dropt a hint of red and gold),
There went about the crooked cavern-caves
Low, flute-like echoes with a noise of wings
And waters flying down far-hidden fells.
Then might be seen the solitary owl,
Perched in the clefts; scared at the coming light,
And staring outward (like a sea-shelled thing
Chased to his cover by some bright fierce foe)
As at a monster in the middle waste.

At last the great kingfisher came and called
Across the hollows loud with early whips.
And lighted, laughing, on the shepherd's hut,
And roused the widow from a swoon like death.

This day, and after it was noised abroad,
By blacks, and straggling horsemen on the roads,
That he was dead " who had been sick so long,"
There flocked a troop from far-surrounding runs

To see their neighbor and to bury him.
And men who had forgotten how to cry
(Rough flinty fellows of the native bush)
Now learned the bitter way, beholding there
The wasted shadow of an iron frame
Brought down so low by years of fearful pain;
And marking, too, the woman's gentle face,
And all the pathos in her moaned reply
Of, "Masters, we have lived in better days."
One stooped — a stockman from the nearer hills —
To loose his wallet-strings, from whence he took
A bag of tea, and laid it on her lap;
Then, sobbing, "God will help you, missus, yet,"
He sought his horse with most bewildered eyes,
And, spurring swiftly, galloped down the glen.

Where black Orara nightly chafes his brink,
Midway between lamenting lines of oak
And Warra's gap, the shepherd's grave was built.
And there the wild-dog pauses, in the midst
Of moonless watches : howling through the gloom
At hopeless shadows flitting to and fro,
What time the east-wind hums his darkest hymn,
And rains beat heavy on the ruined leaf.

There, while the Autumn in the cedar trees
Sat cooped about by cloudy evergreens,
The widow sojourned on the silent road,
And mutely faced the barren mound, and plucked
A straggling shrub from thence, and passed away,
Heart-broken, on to Sydney; where she took

Her passage, in an English vessel bound
To London, for her home of other years.

At rest! Not near, with sorrow on his grave,
And roses quickened into beauty, — wrapt
In all the pathos of perennial bloom;
But far from these, beneath the fretful clay
Of lands within the lone perpetual cry
Of hermit plovers and the night-like oaks,
All moaning for the peace which never comes.

At rest! And she who sits and waits behind
Is in the shadows; but her faith is sure,
And one fine promise of the coming days
Is breaking, like a blessed morning, far
On hills "that slope through darkness up to God."

Henry Kendall.

AUSTRALIA.

Arakoon, the Mountain.

ARAKOON.

LO, in storms, the triple-headed
        Hill, whose dreaded
Bases battle with the seas,
Looms across fierce widths of fleeting
        Waters beating
Evermore on roaring leas!

Arakoon, the black, the lonely!
        Housed with only
Cloud and rain-wind, mist and damp:
Round whose foam-drenched feet, and nether
        Depths, together
Sullen sprites of thunder tramp!

There the East hums loud and surly,
        Late and early,
Through the chasms and the caves:
And across the naked verges
        Leap the surges!
White and wailing waifs of waves.

Day by day, the sea-fogs gathered —
     Tempest-fathered —
Pitch their tents on yonder peak !
Yellow drifts and fragments, lying
     Where the flying
Torrents chafe the cloven creek !

    *   *   *

Ever girt about with noises,
     Stormy voices,
And the salt breath of the strait,
Stands the steadfast Mountain Giant,
     Grim, reliant,
Dark as Death, and firm as Fate !

                          Henry Kendall.

Araluen, the River.

ARALUEN.

RIVER, myrtle-rimmed, and set
     Deep amongst unfooted dells, —
Daughter of gray hills of wet,
     Born by mossed and yellow wells, - -

Now that soft September lays
     Tender hands on thee and thine,
Let me think of blue-eyed days,
     Star-like flowers, and leaves of shine !

Cities soil the life with rust :
     Water-banks are cool and sweet :

River, tired of noise and dust
   Here I come to rest my feet.

Now the month from shade to sun
   Fleets and sings supremest songs,
Now the wilful woodwinds run
   Through the tangled cedar throngs.

Here are cushioned tufts and turns
   Where the sumptuous noontide lies.
Here are seen by flags and ferns
   Summer's large luxurious eyes.

On this spot wan Winter casts
   Eyes of ruth, and spares its green
From his bitter sea-nursed blasts,
   Spears of rain and hailstones keen.

Rather here abideth Spring,
   Lady of a lovely land,
Dear to leaf and fluttering wing,
   Deep in blooms, by breezes fanned.

Faithful friend beyond the main, —
   Friend that Time nor Change makes cold, —
Now, like ghosts, return again
   Pallid perished days of old.

Ah, the days, — the old, old theme
   Never stale, but never new,
Floating, like a pleasant dream,
   Back to me and back to you.

Since we rested on these slopes,
  Seasons fierce have beaten down
Ardent loves and blossoming hopes,
  Loves that lift, and hopes that crown.

But, believe me, still mine eyes
  Often fill with light that springs
From divinity, which lies
  Ever at the heart of things.

Solace do I sometimes find
  Where you used to hear with me
Songs of stream and forest-wind,
  Tones of wave and harp-like tree.

Araluen! home of dreams!
  Fairer for its flowerful glade
Than the face of Persian streams
  Or the slopes of Syrian shade.

Why should I still love it so?
  Friend and brother far away,
Ask the winds that come and go,
  What hath brought me here to-day.

Evermore of you I think,
  When the leaves begin to fall,
Where our river breaks its brink,
  And a rest is over all.

Evermore in quiet lands,
  Friend of mine beyond the sea,
Memory comes with cunning hands,
  Stays, and paints your face for me.

                              Henry Kendall.

Arrawatta, the Glen.

ARRAWATTA.

A SKY of wind! And while these fitful gusts
Are beating round the windows in the cold,
With sullen sobs of rain, behold I shape
A settler's story of the wild old times:
One told by camp-fires when the station-drays
Were housed and hidden, forty years ago;
While swarthy drivers smoked their pipes, and drew,
And crowded round the friendly-gleaming flame
That lured the dingo howling from his caves
And brought sharp sudden feet about the brakes.

A tale of love and death. And shall I say
A tale of love in death; for all the patient eyes
That gathered darkness, watching for a son
And brother, never dreaming of the fate—
The fearful fate he met alone, unknown,
Within the ruthless Australasian wastes?
For, in a far-off sultry summer rimmed
With thunder-cloud and red with forest-fires,
All day, by ways uncouth and ledges rude,
The wild men held upon a stranger's trail
Which ran against the rivers and athwart
The gorges of the deep blue western hills.

And when a cloudy sunset, like the flame
In windy evenings on the Plains of Thirst

Beyond the dead banks of the far Barcoo,
Lay heavy down the topmost peaks, they came
With pent-in breath and stealthy steps, and crouched,
Like snakes, amongst the grasses, till the night
Had covered face from face and thrown the gloom
Of many shadows on the front of things.

There, in the shelter of a nameless glen
Fenced round by cedars and the tangled growths
Of blackwood stained with brown and shot with gray,
The jaded white man built his fire, and turned
His horse adrift amongst the water-pools
That trickled underneath the yellow leaves
And made a pleasant murmur, like the brooks
Of England through the sweet autumnal noons.

Then after he had slaked his thirst, and used
The forest-fare, for which a healthful day
Of mountain-life had brought a zest, he took
His axe, and shaped with boughs and wattle-forks
A wurley, fashioned like a bushman's roof:
The door brought out athwart the strenuous flame:
The back thatched in against a rising wind.

And, while the sturdy hatchet filled the clifts
With sounds unknown, the immemorial haunts
Of echoes sent their lonely dwellers forth
Who lived a life of wonder: flying round
And round the glen, — what time the kangaroo
Leapt from his lair and huddled with the bats, —
Far-scattering down the wildly startled fells.

Then came the doleful owl; and evermore
The bleak morass gave out the bittern's call,
The plover's cry, and many a fitful wail
Of chilly omen, falling on the ear
Like those cold flaws of wind that come and go
An hour before the break of day.

                                        Anon
The stranger held from toil, and, settling down,
He drew rough solace from his well-filled pipe
And smoked into the night: revolving there
The primal questions of a squatter's life;
For in the flats, a short day's journey past
His present camp, his station yards were kept
With many a lodge and paddock jutting forth
Across the heart of unnamed prairie lands,
Now loud with bleating and the cattle bells
And misty with the hut-fire's daily smoke.

Wide spreading flats, and western spurs of hills
That dipped to plains of dim perpetual blue;
Bold summits set against the thunder-heaps;
And slopes be-hacked and crushed by battling kine!
Where now the furious tumult of their feet
Gives back the dust, and up from glen and brake
Evokes fierce clamor, and becomes indeed
A token of the squatter's daring life,
Which growing inland — growing year by year,
Doth set us thinking in these latter days,
And makes one ponder of the lonely kinds
Beyond the lonely tracks of Burke and Wills,
Where, when the wandering Stuart fixed his camps

In central wastes afar from any home
Or haunt of man, and in the changeless midst
Of sullen deserts and the footless miles
Of sultry silence, all the ways about
Grew strangely vocal and a marvellous noise
Became the wonder of the waxing glooms.

*   *   *

Thus passed the time until the moon serene
Stood over high dominion like a dream
Of peace: within the white-transfigured woods,
And o'er the vast dew-dripping wilderness
Of slopes illumined with her silent fires.
Then far beyond the home of pale red leaves
And silver sluices, and the shining stems
Of runnel-blooms, the dreamy wanderer saw,
The wilder for the vision of the moon,
Stark desolations and a waste of plain
All smit by flame and broken with the storms:
Black ghosts of trees, and sapless trunks that stood
Harsh hollow channels of the fiery noise
Which ran from bole to bole a year before,
And grew with ruin, and was like, indeed,
The roar of mighty winds with wintering streams
That foam about the limits of the land,
And mix their swiftness with the flying seas.

Now, when the man had turned his face about
To take his rest, behold the gem-like eyes
Of ambushed wild things stared from bole and brake
With dumb amaze and faint-recurring glance,
And fear anon that drove them down the brush;
While from his den the dingo, like a scout

In sheltered ways, crept out and cowered near
To sniff the tokens of the stranger's feast
And marvel at the shadows of the flame.

Thereafter grew the wind; and chafing depths
In distant waters sent a troubled cry
Across the slumberous forest; and the chill
Of coming rain was on the sleeper's brow.
When, flat as reptiles hutted in the scrub,
A deadly crescent crawled to where he lay, —
A band of fierce fantastic savages
That, starting naked round the faded fire,
With sudden spears and swift terrific yells,
Came bounding wildly at the white man's head,
And faced him, staring like a dream of hell!

Here let me pass! I would not stay to tell
Of hopeless struggles under crushing blows;
Of how the surging fiends with thickening strokes
Howled round the stranger till they drained his
        strength;
How Love and Life stood face to face with Hate
And Death; and then how Death was left alone
With Night and Silence in the sobbing rain.

So, after many moons, the searchers found
The body mouldering in the mouldering dell
Amidst the fungi and the bleaching leaves,
And buried it; and raised a stony mound
Which took the mosses then the place became
The haunt of fearful legends, and the lair
Of bats and adders

                        Henry Kendall.

Coogee.

COOGEE.

SING the song of wave-worn Coogee, — Coogee in the
    distance white
With its jags and points disrupted, gaps and fractures
    fringed with light!
Haunt of gledes and restless plovers of the melancholy
    wail
Ever lending deeper pathos to the melancholy gale.
There, my brothers, down the fissures, chasms deep and
    wan and wild,
Grows the sea-bloom, one that blushes like a shrinking,
    fair, blind child;
And amongst the oozing forelands many a glad green
    rock-vine runs,
Getting ease on earthy ledges sheltered from December
    suns.

Often, when a gusty morning, rising cold and gray and
    strange,
Lifts its face from watery spaces, vistas full with cloudy
    change;
Bearing up a gloomy burden which anon begins to
    wane,
Fading in the sudden shadow of a dark determined
    rain;
Do I seek an eastern window, so to watch the breakers
    beat

Round the steadfast crags of Coogee, dim with drifts
  of driving sleet :
Hearing hollow mournful noises sweeping down a solemn
  shore
While the grim sea-caves are tideless and the storm
  strives at their core.

Often when the floating vapors fill the silent autumn
  leas,
Dreamy memories fall like moonlight over silver, sleeping
  seas,
Youth and I and Love together!—other times and
  other themes
Come to me unsung, unwept for, through the faded
  evening gleams ;
Come to me and touch me mutely,—I that looked and
  longed so well,
Shall I look and yet forget them? who may know or
  who foretell?
Though the southern wind roams, shadowed with its
  immemorial grief,
Where the frosty wings of winter leave their whiteness
  on the leaf?

Friend of mine beyond the waters, here and there these
  perished days
Haunt me with their sweet dead faces and their old
  divided ways.
You that helped and you that loved me, take this song,
  and when you read
Let the lost things come about you, set your thoughts
  and hear and heed :

Time has laid his burden on us : we who wear our
    manhood now, —
We would be the boys we have been, free of heart
    and bright of brow, —
Be the boys for just an hour, with the splendor and
    the speech
Of thy lights and thunders, Coogee, flying up thy
    gleaming beach !

Heart's desire and heart's division ! who would come
    and say to me
With the eyes of far-off friendship, "You are as you
    used to be" ?
Something glad and good has left me here with sick-
    ening discontent,
Tired of looking, neither knowing what it was or
    where it went.
So it is this sight of Coogee, shining in the morning
    dew,
Sets me stumbling through dim summers once on fire
    with youth and you.
Summers pale as southern evenings when the year has
    lost its power,
And the wasted face of April weeps above the withered
    flower.

Not that seasons bring no solace, not that time lacks
    light and rest ;
But the old things were the dearest, and the old loves
    seem the best.
We that start at songs familiar, we that tremble at a
    tone,

Floating down the ways of music, like a sigh of sweet-
    ness flown, —
We can never feel the freshness, never find again the
    mood
Left amongst fair-featured places brightened of our
    brotherhood;
This, and this, we have to think of, when the night
    is over all,
And the woods begin to perish, and the rains begin
    to fall.

Henry Kendall.

———◆◆———

Euroma.

AT EUROMA.

THEY built his mound of the rough red ground,
    By the dip of a desert dell,
Where all things sweet are killed by the heat,
    And scattered o'er flat and fell.
In a burning zone they left him alone,
    Past the uttermost western plain;
And the nightfall dim heard his funeral hymn
    In the voices of wind and rain.

The songs austere of the forests drear,
    And the echoes of clift and cave,
When the dark is keen where the storm hath been,
    Fleet over the far-away grave.
And through the days when the torrid rays
    Strike down on a coppery gloom,

Some spirit grieves in the perished leaves
    Whose theme is that desolate tomb.

No human foot, or paw of brute,
    Halts now where the stranger sleeps;
But cloud and star his fellows are,
    And the rain that sobs and weeps.
The dingo yells by the far iron fells,
    The plover is loud in the range,
But they never come near to the slumberer here,
    Whose rest is a rest without change.

Ah! in his life, had he mother or wife,
    To wait for his step on the floor?
Did Beauty wax dim while watching for him
    Who passed through the threshold no more?
Doth it trouble his head? He is one with the dead;
    He lies by the alien streams;
And sweeter than sleep is death that is deep
    And unvexed by the lordship of dreams.

Henry Kendall.

Illa Creek.

ILLA CREEK.

A STRONG sea-wind flies up and sings
    Across the blown-wet border,
Whose stormy echo runs and rings
    Like bells in wild disorder.

Fierce breath hath vext the foreland's face,
  It glistens, glooms, and glistens;
But deep within this quiet place
  Sweet Illa lies and listens.

Sweet Illa of the shining sands,
  She sleeps in shady hollows
Where August flits with flowerful hands
  And silver Summer follows.

Far up the naked hills is heard
  A noise of many waters;
But green-haired Illa lies unstirred
  Amongst her star-like daughters.

The tempest pent in moaning ways
  Awakes the shepherd yonder;
But Illa dreams, unknown to days
  Whose wings are wind and thunder.

Here fairy hands and floral feet
  Are brought by bright October;
Here stained with grapes, and smit with heat,
  Comes Autumn sweet and sober.

Here lovers rest, what time the red
  And yellow colors mingle,
And daylight droops with dying head
  Beyond the western dingle.

And here, from month to month, the time
  Is kissed by Peace and Pleasure,
While Nature sings her woodland rhyme
  And hoards her woodland treasure.

   *   *   *

Henry Kendall.

Paroo.

ON THE PAROO.

A S when the strong stream of a wintering sea
Rolls round our coast, with bodeful breaks of storm,
And swift salt rain, and bitter wind that saith
Wild things and woeful of the White South Land
Alone with God and Silence in the cold, —
As when this cometh, men from dripping doors
Look forth, and shudder for the mariners
Abroad, so we for absent brothers looked
In days of drought, and when the flying floods
Swept boundless, roaring down the bald, black plains
Beyond the farthest spur of western hills.

For where the Barwan cuts a rotten land,
Or lies unshaken, like a great blind creek,
Between hot mouldering banks, it came to this,
All in a time of short and thirsty sighs,
That thirty rainless months had left the pools
And grass as dry as ashes ; then it was
Our kinsmen started for the lone Paroo,
From point to point, with patient strivings, sheer
Across the horrors of the windless downs,
Blue-gleaming like a sea of molten steel.

But never drought had broke them, never flood
Had quenched them ; they with mighty youth and
  health,

And thews and sinews knotted like the trees, —
They, like the children of the native woods,
Could stem the strenuous waters, or outlive
The crimson days and dull dead nights of thirst
Like camels! yet of what avail was strength
Alone to them — though it was like the rocks
On stormy mountains — in the bloody time
When fierce sleep caught them in the camps at rest,
And violent darkness gripped the life in them
And whelmed them, as an eagle unawares
Is whelmed and slaughtered in a sudden snare?

All murdered by the blacks! smit while they lay
In silver dreams, and with the far faint fall
Of many waters breaking on their sleep!
Yea, in the tracts unknown of any man
Save savages, — the dim-discovered ways
Of footless silence or unhappy winds, —
The wild men came upon them, like a fire
Of desert thunder; and the fine firm lips
That touched a mother's lips a year before,
And hands that knew a dearer hand than life,
Were hewn like sacrifice before the stars,
And left with hooting owls, and blowing clouds,
And falling leaves, and solitary wings!

Ay, you may see their graves, — you who have toiled
And tripped and thirsted, like these men of ours;
For verily I say that not so deep
Their bones are that the scattered drift and dust
Of gusty days will never leave them bare.

O dear, dead, bleaching bones! I know of those
Who have the wild strong will to go and sit
Outside all things with you, and keep the ways
Aloof from bats, and snakes, and trampling feet
That smite your peace and theirs, — who have the heart
Without the lusty limbs to face the fire,
And moonless midnights, and to be indeed,
For very sorrow, like a moaning wind
In wintry forests with perpetual rain.

Henry Kendall.

Pelican Island.

PELICAN ISLAND.

MEANWHILE, not idle, though unwatched by me,
The coral architects in silence reared
Tower after tower beneath the dark abyss.
Pyramidal in form the fabrics rose,
From ample basements narrowing to the height,
Until they pierced the surface of the flood,
And dimpling eddies sparkled round their peaks.
Then (if great things with small may be compared)
They spread like water-lilies, whose broad leaves
Make green and sunny islets on the pool,
For golden flies, on summer days, to haunt,
Safe from the lightning-seizure of the trout;
Or yield their lap to catch the minnow springing

Clear from the stream to 'scape the ruffian pike,
That prowls in disappointed rage beneath,
And wonders where the little wretch found refuge.

One headland topt the waves, another followed;
A third, a tenth, a twentieth soon appeared,
Till the long barren gulf in travail lay
With many an infant struggling into birth.
Larger they grew and lovelier, when they breathed
The vital air, and felt the genial sun;
As though a living spirit dwelt in each,
Which, like the inmate of a flexile shell,
Moulded the shapeless slough with its own motion,
And painted it with colors of the morn.
Amidst that group of younger sisters stood
The Isle of Pelicans, as stands the moon
At midnight, queen among the minor stars,
Differing in splendor, magnitude, and distance.
So looked that sleeping archipelago: small isles,
By interwinding channels linked yet sundered;
All flourishing in peaceful fellowship,
Like forest-oaks that love society:
Of various growth and progress; here, a rock
On which a single palm-tree waved its banner
There, sterile tracts unmouldered into soil;
Yonder, dark woods whose foliage swept the water,
Without a speck of turf, or line of shore,
As though their roots were anchored in the ocean.
But most were gardens redolent with flowers,
And orchards bending with Hesperian fruit
That realized the dreams of olden time.

Throughout this commonwealth of sea-sprung lands
Life kindled in ten thousand happy forms;
Earth, air, and ocean were all full of life,
Still highest in the rank of being soared
The fowls amphibious, and the inland tribes
Of dainty plumage or melodious song;
In gaudy robes of many-colored patches,
The parrots swung like blossoms on the trees,
While their harsh voices undeceived the ear.
More delicately pencilled, finer drawn
In shape and lineament, — too exquisite
For gross delights, — the Birds of Paradise
Floated aloof, as though they lived on air,
And were the orient progeny of heaven,
Or spirits made perfect veiled in shining raiment.
From flower to flower, where wild bees flew and sung,
As countless, small, and musical as they,
Showers of bright humming-birds came down, and
    plied
The same ambrosial task, with slender bills
Extracting honey, hidden in those bells
Whose richest blooms grew pale beneath the blaze
Of twinkling winglets hovering o'er their petals,
Brilliant as rain-drops where the western sun
Sees his own beams of miniature in each.

      *   *   *

The fierce sea-eagle, humble in attire,
In port terrific, from his lonely eyrie,
(Itself a burden for the tallest tree)
Looked down o'er land and sea as his dominions:
Now, from long chase, descending with his prey,

Young seal or dolphin, in his deadly clutch,
He fed his eagles in the noonday sun;
Nor less at midnight ranged the deep for game;
At length entrapped with his own talons, struck
Too deep to be withdrawn, where a strong shark,
Roused by the anguish, with impetuous plunge,
Dragged his assailant down into the abyss,
Struggling in vain for liberty and life:
His young ones heard their parent's dying shrieks,
And watched in vain for his returning wing.

Here ran the stormy-petrels on the waves,
As though they were the shadows of themselves
Reflected from a loftier flight through space.
The stern and gloomy raven haunted here,
A hermit of the atmosphere, on land
Among vociferating crowds a stranger,
Whose hoarse, low, ominous croak disclaimed communion
nion
With those upon the offal of whose meals
He gorged alone, or tore their own rank corses.
The heavy penguin, neither fish nor fowl,
With scaly feathers and with finny wings,
Plumped stone-like from the rock into the gulf,
Rebounding upward swift as from a sling.
Through yielding water as through limpid air,
The cormorant, Death's living arrow, flew,
Nor ever missed a stroke, or dealt a second,
So true the infallible destroyer's aim.

James Montgomery.

VAN DIEMEN'S LAND (TASMANIA).

D'ENTRECASTEAUX CHANNEL.

NOW D'Entrecasteaux Channel opens fair,
    And Tasman's Head lies on your starboard bow
Huge rocks and stunted trees meet you where'er
    You look around; 'tis a bold coast enow.
With foul wind and crank ship 't were hard to wear:
    A reef of rocks lies westward long and low.
At ebb tide you may see the Actæon lie
A sheer hulk o'er the breakers, high and dry.

'T is a most beauteous Strait. The Great South Sea's
    Proud waves keep holiday along its shore,
And as the vessel glides before the breeze,
    Broad bays and isles appear, and steep cliffs hoar
With groves on either hand of ancient trees
    Planted by Nature in the days of yore :
Van Dieman's on the left and Bruné's isle
Forming the starboard shore for many a mile.

But all is still as death ! Nor voice of man
    Is heard, nor forest warbler's tuneful song.
It seems as if this beauteous world began
    To be but yesterday, and the earth still young

And unpossessed. For though the tall black swan
  Sits on her nest and stately sails along,
And the green wild doves their fleet pinions ply,
And the gray eagle tempts the azure sky,

Yet all is still as death! Wild solitude
  Reigns undisturbed along that voiceless shore,
And every tree seems standing as it stood
  Six thousand years ago. The loud wave's roar
Were music in these wilds. The wise and good
  That wont of old, as hermits, to adore
The God of Nature in the desert drear,
Might sure have found a fit sojourning here.

John Dunmore Lang.

NEW ZEALAND, NEW GUINEA, AND NEW CALEDONIA.

THE THREE ISLANDS.

HERE lifts New Zealand, mid a sea of storms,
Her hills that threaten heaven like Titan forms,—
Where the long lizard on the herbage lies,
And clouds of emerald beauty paint the skies;
Where the dark savage courts the burning noon,
And counts his epochs by the hundredth moon!
And yonder, redolent with fruits and flowers,
With spicy gales and aromatic showers,
And shady palms that into mid-air run,
To meet the wingéd creatures of the sun,
Fair Papua calls upon the mourning muse
To pause and weep above the lost Pérouse!
But vain her wailing, as the toil was vain
That sought this second Hylas o'er the main!
Eastward she turns, where many an island smiles,
Each like a chief amid its vassal isles,
Where lie the lands so often lost and found,
And where, so long in circling silence bound,
New Caledonia sits upon the seas
That roll their waves amid the Cyclades!

Thomas Kibble Hervey.

ASIATIC ISLANDS.

THE INDIAN ARCHIPELAGO.

BENEATH the spreading wings of purple morn,
Behold what isles these glistening seas adorn!
Mid hundreds yet unnamed, Ternat behold;
By day her hills in pitchy clouds enrolled,
By night like rolling waves the sheets of fire
Blaze o'er the seas, and high to heaven aspire.
For Lusian hands here blooms the fragrant clove,
But Lusian blood shall sprinkle every grove.
The golden birds that ever sail the skies,
Here to the sun display their shining dyes,
Each want supplied, on air they ever soar;
The ground they touch not till they breathe no more
Here Banda's isles their fair embroidery spread
Of various fruitage, azure, white, and red;
And birds of every beauteous plume display
Their glittering radiance, as from spray to spray,
From bower to bower, on busy wings they rove,
To seize the tribute of the spicy grove.

Borneo here expands her ample breast,
By Nature's hand in woods of camphire dressed;
The precious liquid weeping from the trees
Glows warm with health, the balsam of disease.
Fair are Timora's dales with groves arrayed;
Each rivulet murmurs in the fragrant shade,
And in its crystal breast displays the bowers
Of sanders, blessed with health-restoring powers.
Where to the south the world's broad surface bends,
Lo, Sunda's realm her spreading arms extends.
From hence the pilgrim brings the wondrous tale,
A river groaning through a dreary dale,
For all is stone around, converts to stone
Whate'er of verdure in its breast is thrown.
Lo, gleaming blue o'er fair Sumatra's skies,
Another mountain's trembling flames arise;
Here from the trees the gum all fragrance swells,
And softest oil a wondrous fountain wells.
Nor these alone the happy isle bestows,
Fine is her gold, her silk resplendent glows.
Wide forests there beneath Maldivia's tide
From withering air their wondrous fruitage hide.
The green-haired Nereids tend the bowery dells,
Whose wondrous fruitage poisoned rage expels.
In Ceylon, lo, how high yon mountain's brows!
The sailing clouds its middle height enclose.
Holy the hill is deemed, the hallowed tread
Of sainted footstep marks its rocky head.
Laved by the Red-Sea gulf, Socotra's bowers
There boast the tardy aloe's clustered flowers.

Luis de Camoens. Tr. W. J. Mickle.

POLYNESIA.

Pelew Islands.

ABBA THULE.

I CLIMB the highest cliff: I hear the sound
Of dashing waves; I gaze intent around:
I mark the sun that orient lifts his head!
I mark the sea's lone rule beneath him spread:
But not a speck can my long-straining eye,
A shadow, o'er the tossing waste descry,
That I might weep tears of delight, and say,
"It is the bark that bore my child away!"

Thou sun, that beamest bright, beneath whose eye
The worlds unknown, and outstretched waters, lie,
Dost thou behold him now? On some rude shore,
Around whose crags the cheerless billows roar,
Watching the unwearied surges doth he stand,
And think upon his father's distant land?
Or has his heart forgot, so far away,
These native scenes, these rocks and torrents gray,
The tall bananas whispering to the breeze,
The shores, the sound of these encircling seas,

Heard from his infant days, and the piled heap
Of holy stones, where his forefathers sleep?

Ah me! till sunk by sorrow, I shall dwell
With them forgetful.in the narrow cell,
Never shall time from my fond heart efface
His image; oft his shadow I shall trace
Upon the glimmering waters, when on high
The white moon wanders through the cloudless sky.
Oft in my silent cave (when to its fire
From the night's rushing tempest we retire)
I shall behold his form, his aspect bland;
I shall retrace his footsteps in the sand;
And, when the hollow-sounding surges swell,
Still think I listen to his echoing shell.

*   *   *

O, I shall never, never hear his voice;
The spring-time shall return, the isles rejoice;
But faint and weary I shall meet the morn,
And mid the cheering sunshine droop forlorn!

The joyous conch sounds in the high wood loud,
O'er all the beach now stream the busy crowd;
Fresh breezes stir the waving plantain grove;
The fisher carols in the winding cove;
And light canoes along the lucid tide
With painted shells and sparkling paddles glide.
I linger on the desert rock alone,
Heartless, and cry for thee, my son, my son.

William Lisle Bowles.

Pitcairn's Island.

A SONG OF PITCAIRN'S ISLAND.

COME, take our boy, and we will go
    Before our cabin-door;
The winds shall bring us, as they blow,
    The murmurs of the shore;
And we will kiss his young blue eyes,
And I will sing him, as he lies,
    Songs that were made of yore;
I 'll sing, in his delighted ear,
The island lays thou lov'st to hear.

And thou, while stammering I repeat,
    Thy country's tongue shalt teach;
'T is not so soft, but far more sweet,
    Than my own native speech:
For thou no other tongue didst know,
When, scarcely twenty moons ago,
    Upon Tahete's beach,
Thou cam'st to woo me to be thine,
With many a speaking look and sign.

I knew thy meaning, — thou didst praise
    My eyes, my locks of jet;
Ah! well for me they won thy gaze, —
    But thine were fairer yet!
I 'm glad to see my infant wear
Thy soft blue eyes and sunny hair,
    And when my sight is met

By his white brow and blooming cheek,
I feel a joy I cannot speak.

Come talk of Europe's maids with me,
    Whose necks and cheeks, they tell,
Outshine the beauty of the sea,
    White foam and crimson shell.
I 'll shape like theirs my simple dress,
And bind like them each jetty tress, —
    A sight to please thee well;
And for my dusky brow will braid
A bonnet like an English maid.

Come, for the soft low sunlight calls,
    We lose the pleasant hours;
'T is lovelier than these cottage walls,
    That seat among the flowers.
And I will learn of thee a prayer,
To Him, who gave a home so fair,
    A lot so blessed as ours, —
The God who made, for thee and me,
This sweet lone isle amid the sea.

William Cullen Bryant.

Sandwich Islands.

THE EARL OF SANDWICH.

THEY called the islands by his name,
    Those isles, the far away and fair;
A graceful fancy linked with fame,
A flattery — such as poets' are,

Who link with lovely things their praise,
And ask the earth, and ask the sky,
To color with themselves their lays,
And some associate grace supply.

But here it was a sailor's thought,
That named the island from the earl,
That dreams of England might be brought
To those soft shores and seas of pearl.

How very fair they must have seemed
When first they darkened on the deep!
Like all the wandering seaman dreamed,
When land rose lovely on his sleep.

How many dreams they turned to truth
When first they met the sailor's eyes;
Green with the sweet earth's southern youth,
And azure with her southern skies.

And yet our English thought beguiles
The mariner where'er he roam;
He looks upon the new-found isles,
And calls them by some name of home.

Letitia Elizabeth Landon.

HAWAII.

AN ocean-planet, rounded by a glory,
The billowy glory of the great Pacific,
Withdrawn in spheres remote of rolling blue.

An island, central with inferior groupings,
Like Jupiter, in the cerulean distance,
Magnificent among his circling moons.

Planet-like poiséd half submerged in ocean :
One hemisphere above the water-level
Apparent, belted by three climate-zones.

The heavy mango droops, the slim palm towers,
By intertropical shores; gleam silver summits
(Through wind-clouds) Arctic with eternal frost.

Crowned with the vast white dome of Mauna Loa,
Escarpments rich with the pandanus, ravines,
Cascades and rainbows, form thy globular shell.

A hollow globe ; beneath the snow, the verdure,
The ambient ocean, live, primordial fires,
Which have created, dwell — and may destroy.

    *   *   *

Hush, — hence the theme! 'T is torrid noon, with
    freshness
On lake and waterfall, soft vowels and laughter
From brown amphibious girls in Eden's guise.

And, as I gaze and write, glorious Hawáii!
I see no terror in thy soaring beauty,
Thy sky of lazuli and sapphire sea.

William Gibson.

Tonga (Friendly) Islands.

SONG OF THE TONGA-ISLANDERS.

HOW pleasant were the songs of Toobonai,
  When summer's sun went down the coral bay!
Come, let us to the islet's softest shade,
And hear the warbling birds! the damsels said:
The wood-dove from the forest depth shall coo,
Like voices of the gods from Bolotoo;
We'll cull the flowers that grow above the dead,
For these most bloom where rests the warrior's head;
And we will sit in twilight's face, and see
The sweet moon dancing through the tooa 'tree.
The lofty accents of whose sighing bough
Shall sadly please us as we lean below;
Or climb the steep, and view the surf in vain
Wrestle with rocky giants o'er the main,
Which spurn in columns back the baffled spray.
How beautiful are these, how happy they,
Who, from the toil and tumult of their lives,
Steal to look down where naught but ocean strives!
Even he too loves at times the blue lagoon,
And smooths his ruffled mane beneath the moon.

Yes—from the sepulchre we'll gather flowers,
Then feast like spirits in their promised bowers,
Then plunge and revel in the rolling surf,
Then lay our limbs along the tender turf,

And, wet and shining from the sportive toil,
Anoint our bodies with the fragrant oil,
And plait our garlands gathered from the grave,
And wear the wreaths that sprung from out the brave.
But lo! night comes, the Moon wooes us back,
The sound of mats is heard along our track;
Anon the torchlight-dance shall fling its sheen
In flashing mazes o'er the Marly's green;
And we too will be there; we too recall
The memory bright with many a festival,
Ere Fiji blew the shell of war, when foes
For the first time were wafted in canoes.
Alas! for them the flower of mankind bleeds;
Alas! for them our fields are rank with weeds.

Forgotten is the rapture, or unknown,
Of wandering with the moon and love alone.
But be it so, — they taught us how to wield
The club, and rain our arrows o'er the field;
Now let them reap the harvest of their art!
But feast to-night! to-morrow we depart.
Strike up the dance, the cava-bowl fill high,
Drain every drop! — to-morrow we may die.
In summer garments be our limbs arrayed;
Around our waist the Tappa's white displayed;
Thick wreaths shall form our coronal, like spring's,
And round our necks shall glance the Hooni strings;
So shall their brighter hues contrast the glow
Of the dusk bosoms that beat high below.

But now the dance is o'er — yet stay awhile;
Ah, pause! nor yet put out the social smile.

To-morrow for the Moon we depart,
But not to-night, - to-night is for the heart.
Again bestow the wreaths we gently woo,
Ye young enchantresses of gay Licoo!
How lovely are your forms! how every sense
Bows to your beauties, softened, but intense,
Like to the flowers on Mataloco's steep,
Which fling their fragrance far athwart the deep
We too will see Licoo: but oh, my heart —
What do I say? to-morrow we depart.

Lord Byron.

SONG OF THE TONGA-ISLANDERS.

COME to Licoo! the sun is riding
  Down hills of gold to his coral bowers;
Come where the wood-pigeon's moan is chiding
The song of the wind, while we gather flowers.

Let us plait the garland, and weave the staves,
While the wild waves dance on our iron strand,
To-morrow these waves may wash our graves,
And the moon look down on a ruined land.

Let us light the torches, and dip our hair
In the fragrant oil of the sandal tree;
Strike the bonjoo, and the oola share,
Ere the death-gods hear our jubilee.

Who are they that in floating towers
Come with their skins of curdled snows?

They shall see our maidens dress our bowers,
While the hooni shines on their sunny brows.

Who shall mourn when, red with slaughter,
Finow sits on the funeral stone?
Who shall weep for his dying daughter?
Who shall answer the red chief's moan?

He shall cry unheard by the funeral stone,
He shall sink unseen by the split canoe,
Though the plantain-bird be his alone,
And the thundering gods of Fanfonnoo.

Let us not think 't is but an hour
Ere the wreath shall drop from the warrior's waist;
Let us not think 't is but an hour
We have on our perfumed mats to waste.

Shall we not banquet, though Tonga's king
To-morrow may hurl the battle-spear?
Let us whirl our torches, and tread the ring, —
He only shall find our footprints here.

We will dive, — and the turtle's track shall guide
Our way to the cave where Hoonga dwells,
Where under the tide he hides his bride,
And lives by the light of its starry shells.

Come to Licoo! in yellow skies
The sun shines bright, and the wild waves play;
To-morrow for us may never rise; —
Come to Licoo to-day, to-day.

Anonymous.

THE REVENGE.

A BALLAD OF THE FLEET, 1591.

AT Flores in the Azores Sir Richard Grenville lay,
  And a pinnace, like a fluttered bird, came flying
    from far away :
"Spanish ships of war at sea! we have sighted fifty-
    three !"
Then sware Lord Thomas Howard: "'Fore God I am
  no coward ;
But I cannot meet them here, for my ships are out
  of gear,
And the half my men are sick. I must fly, but follow
  quick.
We are six ships of the line; can we fight with fifty-
  three ?"

Then spake Sir Richard Grenville: "I know you are
  no coward ;
You fly them for a moment to fight with them again.

But I've ninety men and more that are lying sick
        ashore.
I should count myself the coward if I left them, my
        Lord Howard,
To these Inquisition dogs and the devildoms of Spain."

So Lord Howard past away with five ships of war that
        day,
Till he melted like a cloud in the silent summer heaven;
But Sir Richard bore in hand all his sick men from the
        land
Very carefully and slow,
Men of Bidford in Devon,
And we laid them on the ballast down below;
For we brought them all aboard,
And they blest him in their pain, that they were not
        left to Spain,
To the thumbscrew and the stake, for the glory of the
        Lord.

He had only a hundred seamen to work the ship and
        to fight,
And he sailed away from Flores till the Spaniard came
        in sight,
With his huge sea-castles heaving upon the weather
        bow.
" Shall we fight or shall we fly?
Good Sir Richard, let us know,
For to fight is but to die!
There'll be little of us left by the time the sun be set."
And Sir Richard said again: " We be all good Eng-
        lishmen.

Let us bang these dogs of Seville, the children of the
    devil,
For I never turned my back upon Don or devil yet."

Sir Richard spoke, and he laughed, and we roared a
    hurrah, and so
The little "Revenge" ran on sheer into the heart of
    the foe,
With her hundred fighters on deck, and her ninety sick
    below ;
For half of their fleet to the right and half to the left
    were seen,
And the little "Revenge" ran on through the long sea-
    lane between.

Thousands of their soldiers looked down from their
    decks and laughed.
Thousands of their seamen made mock at the mad
    little craft
Running on and on, till delayed
By their mountain-like "San Philip" that, of fifteen
    hundred tons,
And up-shadowing high above us with her yawning
    tiers of guns,
Took the breath from our sails, and we stayed.

And while now the great "San Philip" hung above
    us like a cloud
Whence the thunderbolt will fall
Long and loud,
Four galleons drew away

From the Spanish fleet that day,
And two upon the larboard and two upon the star-
board lay,
And the battle-thunder broke from them all.

But anon the great " San Philip," she bethought herself and went,
Having that within her womb that had left her ill-
content ;
And the rest they came aboard us, and they fought us
hand to hand,
For a dozen times they came with their pikes and mus-
queteers,
And a dozen times we shook 'em off as a dog that
shakes his ears
When he leaps from the water to the land.

And the sun went down, and the stars came out far
over the summer sea,
But never a moment ceased the fight of the one and
the fifty-three.
Ship after ship, the whole night long, their high-built
galleons came,
Ship after ship, the whole night long, with her battle-
thunder and flame ;
Ship after ship, the whole night long, drew back with
her dead and her shame;
For some were sunk and many were shattered, and so
could fight us no more —
God of battles, was ever a battle like this in the world
before ?

For he said, " Fight on! fight on!"
Though his vessel was all but a wreck;
And it chanced that, when half of the summer night
     was gone,
With a grisly wound to be dressed he had left the
     deck,
But a bullet struck him that was dressing it suddenly
     dead,
And himself he was wounded again in the side and
     the head,
And he said, " Fight on! fight on!"

And the night went down, and the sun smiled out far
     over the summer sea,
And the Spanish fleet with broken sides lay round us
     all in a ring;
But they dared not touch us again, for they feared
     that we still could sting,
So they watched what the end would be.
And we had not fought them in vain,
But in perilous plight were we,
Seeing forty of our poor hundred were slain,
And half of the rest of us maimed for life
In the crash of the cannonades and the desperate strife;
And the sick men down in the hold were most of them
     stark and cold,
And the pikes were all broken or bent, and the powder
     was all of it spent;
And the masts and the rigging were lying over the side;
But Sir Richard cried in his English pride,
" We have fought such a fight for a day and a night

As may never be fought again!
We have won great glory, my men!
And a day less or more
At sea or ashore,
We die — does it matter when?
Sink me the ship, Master Gunner — sink her, split
her in twain!
Fall into the hands of God, not into the hands of
Spain!"

And the gunner said, "Ay, ay," but the seamen made
reply:
"We have children, we have wives,
And the Lord hath spared our lives;
We will make the Spaniard promise, if we yield, to
let us go;
We shall live to fight again and to strike another blow."
And the lion there lay dying, and they yielded to the
foe.

And the stately Spanish men to their flagship bore
him then,
Where they laid him by the mast, old Sir Richard
caught at last,
And they praised him to his face with their courtly
foreign grace;
But he rose upon their decks, and he cried:
"I have fought for Queen and Faith like a valiant
man and true;
I have only done my duty as a man is bound to do:
With a joyful spirit I, Sir Richard Grenville, die!"

And he fell upon their decks, and he died
And they stared at the dead that had been so valiant
and true,
And had holden the power and glory of Spain so cheap,
That he dared her with one little ship and his Eng-
lish few;
Was he devil or man? He was devil for aught they
knew,
But they sank his body with honor down into the deep,
And they manned the "Revenge" with a swarthier
alien crew,
And away she sailed with her loss and longed for her
own;
When a wind from the lands they had ruined awoke
from sleep,
And the water began to heave and the weather to moan,
And or ever that evening ended a great gale blew,
And a wave like the wave that is raised by an earth-
quake grew,
Till it smote on their hulls and their sails and their
masts and their flags,
And the whole sea plunged and fell on the shot-shat-
tered navy of Spain,
And the little "Revenge" herself went down by the
island crags
To be lost evermore in the main.

                                     Alfred Tennyson.

Bermudas.

BERMUDA.

BERMUDA, walled with rocks, who does not know?
That happy island where huge lemons grow,
And orange-trees, which golden fruit do bear,
The Hesperian garden boasts of none so fair;
Where shining pearl, coral, and many a pound,
On the rich shore, of ambergris is found.
The lofty cedar, which to heaven aspires,
The prince of trees! is fuel to their fires;
The smoke by which their loaded spits do turn,
For incense might on sacred altars burn;
Their private roofs on odorous timber borne,
Such as might palaces for kings adorn.
The sweet palmettos a new Bacchus yield,
With leaves as ample as the broadest shield,
Under the shadow of whose friendly boughs
They sit, carousing where their liquor grows.
Figs there unplanted through the fields do grow,
Such as fierce Cato did the Romans show,
With the rare fruit inviting them to spoil
Carthage, the mistress of so rich a soil.
The naked rocks are not unfruitful there,
But, at some constant seasons, every year,
Their barren tops with luscious food abound,
And with the eggs of various fowls are crowned.
Tobacco is the worst of things, which they

To English landlords, as their tribute, pay.
Such is the mould, that the blessed tenant feeds
On precious fruits, and pays his rent in weeds.
With candied plantains, and the juicy pine,
On choicest melons, and sweet grapes, they dine,
And with potatoes fat their wanton swine.
Nature these cates, with such a lavish hand,
Pours out among them, that our coarser land
Tastes of that bounty, and does cloth return,
Which not for warmth, but ornament, is worn;
For the kind spring, which but salutes us here,
Inhabits there, and courts them all the year.
Ripe fruits and blossoms on the same trees live;
At once they promise what at once they give.
So sweet the air, so moderate the clime,
None sickly lives, or dies before his time.
Heaven sure has kept this spot of earth uncursed,
To show how all things were created first.

Edmund Waller.

SONG OF THE EMIGRANTS IN BERMUDA.

WHERE the remote Bermudas ride
In the ocean's bosom unespied,
From a small boat that rowed along
The listening winds received this song:

" What should we do but sing His praise,
That led us through the watery maze
Where he the huge sea-monsters wracks,
That lift the deep upon their backs,

"Unto an isle so long unknown,
And yet far kinder than our own?
He lands us on a grassy stage,
Safe from the storms, and prelate's rage:

"He gave us this eternal spring
Which here enamels everything,
And sends the fowls to us in care
On daily visits through the air.

"He hangs in shades the orange bright,
Like golden lamps in the green night,
And does in the pomegranates close
Jewels more rich than Ormus shows:

"He makes the figs our mouths to meet,
And throws the melons at our feet;
But apples, plants of such a price,
No tree could ever bear them twice.

"With cedars chosen by his hand
From Lebanon he stores the land;
And makes the hollow seas that roar
Proclaim the ambergris on shore.

"He cast (of which we rather boast)
The Gospel's pearl upon our coast;
And in these rocks for us did frame
A temple where to sound his name.

"O, let our voice his praise exalt
Till it arrive at heaven's vault,

Which then perhaps rebounding may
Echo beyond the Mexique bay."

Thus sung they in the English boat
A holy and a cheerful note:
And all the way, to guide their chime,
With falling oars they kept the time.

Andrew Marvell.

Canary Islands.

THE CANARIES.

DIM he discerns majestic Atlas rise,
And bend beneath the burden of the skies, —
His towering brows aloft no tempests know,
Whilst lightning flies and thunder rolls below
  Distant from hence, beyond a waste of plains,
Proud Teneriffe, his giant brother, reigns:
With breathing fire his pitchy nostrils glow,
As from his sides he shakes the fleecy snow.
Around this hoary prince, from watery beds,
His subject islands raise their verdant heads;
The waves so gently wash each rising hill,
The land seems floating,   and the ocean, still
  Eternal spring, with smiling verdure, here
Warms the mild air, and crowns the youthful year;
From crystal rocks transparent riv'lets flow;
The tuberose ever breathes, and violets blow;

The vine, undressed, her swelling clusters bears;
The laboring hind the mellow olive cheers;
Blossoms and fruit, at once, the citron shows,
And, as she pays, discovers still she owes;
The orange to her sun her pride displays,
And gilds her fragrant apples with his rays;
No blasts e'er discompose the peaceful sky,
The springs but murmur, and the winds but sigh:
The tuneful swans on gliding rivers float,
And, warbling dirges, die on every note:
Where Flora treads, her zephyr garlands flings,
And scatters odors from his purple wings,
Whilst birds, from woodbine bowers and jasmine groves,
Chant their glad nuptials and unenvied loves.
Mild seasons, rising hills, and silent dales,
Cool grottos, silver brooks, and flowery vales,
Groves filled with balmy shrubs, in pomp appear,
And scent with gales of sweets the circling year.

Sir Samuel Garth.

TENERIFFE.

MOTHER of musings, Contemplation sage,
Whose grotto stands upon the topmost rock
Of Teneriffe: mid the tempestuous night,
On which, in calmest meditation held,
Thou hear'st with howling winds the beating rain
And drifting hail descend; or if the skies
Unclouded shine, and through the blue serene
Pale Cynthia rolls her silver-axled car,
Whence gazing steadfast on the spangled vault

Raptured thou sitt'st, while murmurs indistinct
Of distant billows soothe thy pensive ear
With hoarse and hollow sounds; secure, self-blest,
There oft thou listen'st to the wild uproar
Of fleets encountering, that in whispers low
Ascends the rocky summit, where thou dwell'st
Remote from man, conversing with the spheres!

Thomas Warton.

THE BIRD OF THE CANARIES.

The canary, in its native woods, is of a greenish color, and is an inferior songster. It is said to acquire its beautiful yellow hue and rich song by domestication in colder latitudes.

THEY say that island-bird, that sings
  Within our homes so rich a song, —
The little bird with golden wings,
  That poureth, all day long,
A flute-like music, sweet and clear,
  As if it were a spirit's lay,
That brought the tones to mortal ear
  Of fay-land, far away,
The small bright bird that cometh west,
From the blue islands of the blest,
They say that, in its own warm bowers,
Where that fair songster floateth, free
As floats the breeze o'er all the flowers
  That scent the tropic sea,
The sun it soars to, fails to fling
This golden gleam upon its wing.

That seemeth as it drew its dyes
From wandering through those burning skies;
The sun it sings to, shines in vain
To wake that wild and witching strain
That gushes forth to meet his smiles,
Like incense, from our colder isles, —
The sweet and swelling music calls
That answer where the daybeam falls,
As if its touch had power to start
Some spring within the minstrel's heart,
And play those wingéd lyres of gold
As erst it played the Memnon old;
That these its fairy hues belong
To wing restrained and riper age,
And still it pours its sweetest song
Within its northern cage, —
And, in its gifts most precious, comes
To bless us, in our human homes!

O fairy from the far-off main!
Thou little flute with golden wings!
Thy spirit-hue and spirit-strain
Are types of fairer things,
And we have dearer gifts than these
Amid the mists of northern seas!
Bright forms that flutter in the sun,
With voices sweet as silver bells,
Whose tones along the spirit run
Like music's very spells, —
And open, with their own sweet art,
Those inner chambers of the heart,

Within whose depths was never heard
The singing of the bird.
And if thy wing of gold or green
Be not to our beloved given,
Winged thoughts, within their dark eyes seen,
Take oft the soul to heaven,
But bring it surely back, to rest,
At eve, within an earthly nest.
Our fairies these, — while floating, free
As thou amid thy far-off sea,
And, like thy sisters, singing sooth,
In the bright island of their youth!
But years to our beloved bring
A richer song, with riper age,
When each is bound, with golden ring,
Within a golden cage, —
In whose sweet hush and holy rest
New sounds steal up along the breast, —
The angels playing soft and low,
As erst in Eden, long ago,
Rich harmonies, till then unheard,
Gush from our own bright human bird,
And hues come o'er its heart, whose dyes
Can have no fountain but the skies!
O, beauty haunteth everywhere,
For spirits that can see aright,
And music fills the common air
Of morn and noon and night;
But beauty wears no form on earth
Like that which sitteth by the hearth;
And, mid the music of the throng,

They never know, who always roam,
How sweeter far that sweetest song
That woman sings — at home.

Thomas Kibble Hervey.

DIRGE ON GUILLEN PERAZA,

GOVERNOR OF THE CANARIES, WHO FELL IN ATTEMPTING
THE CONQUEST OF THE ISLAND PALMA, SOON AFTER THE
YEAR 1814.

PERAZA, virgins fair and chaste
    Wail, as you wish for heaven to smile!
That flower of youth has faded fast,
That lovely flower, too fair to last,
    Lies withered in wild Palma's Isle.

The Palm no more shalt thou be styled,
    Thou scene of dire disgrace and shame!
Thy name shall be the Bramble wild,
The Cypress sad by death defiled,
    That sunk so dear a chieftain's fame!

May dire volcanoes waste thy plains,
    Pleasures desert thy guilty land,
Be haunted still by woes and pains,
And still, for spring's reviving rains,
    Thy flowery fields o'erwhelmed with sand!

Peraza! where is now thy shield?
    Peraza! where is now thy spear?

No more his lance the chief shall wield,
His broken weapons strew the field :
    Alas, for victory bought so dear !
                From the Spanish.   Tr. John Leyden.

TENERIFFE.

THERE is an isle which I have seen,
    Whose slopes and vales are fadeless green,
Whose flowers are evermore in bloom,
And all whose seasons breathe perfume, —
The fairest of the Happy Isles
Whereon eternal summer smiles.
There the dark cypress rears its spire
Against the sunset's tropic fire ;
There the palm lifts its bronze-like shaft
Slow-rocking when the sea-winds waft
The caprioté's song of love
Where black-eyed Spanish maidens rove
And roses cull for festal days,
And on the passing wanderer gaze
With glances passionate and keen,
Yet full of tenderness, I ween.

The lizard basks upon the walls
Whereon the yellow sunlight falls,
Or darts amid the cactus' spines,
Or where the purple-loaded vines
Over the trellis weave a bower,
And deck the gray, embattled tower.

Around the isle volcanic capes,
In huge and castellated shapes,
And ruddy rocks grotesque and weird,
Like giants of the deep are reared;
While age to age, forevermore,
The surges roll with sullen roar
Upon the lava-laden shore.
Enthroned on precipices grand,
Serene above that summer land,
Gray Teneriffe in solitude
Commands the ocean's mighty flood,
And his fire-riven breast enshrouds
With the majestic pomp of clouds,
While from the crater-peak on high,
Outlined stupendous in the sky,
Fair wreaths of mist perpetual rise,
Like daily smoke of sacrifice
Burned to the immortals in the skies.
But when the sun draws near the verge
Of the receding westering surge,
O, then across the eastern sea, —
Like shadow of eternity, —
Impalpable, mysterious, vast,
The shadow of the Peak is cast,
A purple mist against the arch
Through which the constellations march,
Until Night's curtains are unfurled,
And darkness veils the sleeping world.
The music of the sea-beat shores
Up through the silent twilight soars,
In eerie, plaintive requiem lay

For a lost race long past away,
A pastoral race whose bones were laid
In the dread cavern's sunless shade;[1]
Thy mystic murmurs soft and low
By the old patriarch gently flow, —
The dragon-tree whose crest upbears
The burden of three thousand years.
By pathways where the ocean laves
Their footsteps with its harmless waves,
The islesmen in procession wend,
Or over craggy mountains tend,
To dance about the virgin's shrine
While maidens form in merry line
And hail the shimmering evening star
With tinkle of the blithe guitar.
The chime from ancient campaniles
O'er lovely Orotava steals;
From slope to slope the music swells,
Till Realejo's silvery bells
Respond among the mountain dells,
And all the fragrant evening air
Repeats the melody of prayer.

Seymour Green Wheeler Benjamin

---

[1] The Guanches, who were always embalmed and buried in almost inaccessible caves. They were finally exterminated by the Spaniards

Coral Reefs and Islands.

THE CORAL ISLAND.

I saw the living pile ascend,
The mausoleum of its architects,
Still dying upwards as their labors closed :
Slime the material, but the slime was turned
To adamant by their petrific touch ;
Frail were their frames, ephemeral their lives,
Their masonry imperishable. All
Life's needful functions, food, exertion, rest,
By nice economy of Providence
Were overruled to carry on the process
Which out of water brought forth solid rock.

Atom by atom thus the burden grew,
Even like an infant in the womb, till Time
Delivered Ocean of that monstrous birth, —
A coral island, stretching east and west,
In God's own language to its parent saying,
"Thus far, nor farther, shalt thou go ; and here
Shall thy proud waves be stayed." A point at first,
It peered above those waves ; a point so small
I just perceived it, fixed where all was floating ;
And when a bubble crossed it, the blue film
Expanded, like a sky above the speck.
That speck became a hand-breadth ; day and night
It spread, accumulated, and erelong

Presented to my view a dazzling plain,
White as the moon amid the sapphire sea;
Bare at low water, and as still as death;
But when the tide came gurgling o'er the surface,
'T was like a resurrection of the dead.
From graves innumerable, punctures fine
In the close coral, capillary swarms
Of reptiles, horrent as Medusa's snakes,
Covered the bald-pate reef; then all was life
And indefatigable industry;
The artisans were twisting to and-fro
In idle-seeming convolutions, yet
They never vanished with the ebbing surge,
Till pellicle on pellicle, and layer
On layer, was added to the growing mass.
Erelong the reef o'ertopt the spring flood's height,
And mocked the billows when they leaped upon it.
Unable to maintain their slippery hold,
And falling down in foam-wreaths round its verge
Steep were the flanks, with precipices sharp,
Descending to their base in ocean-gloom
Chasms, few and narrow and irregular,
Formed harbors safe at once and perilous, —
Safe for defence, but perilous to enter.
A sea-lake shone amidst the fossil isle,
Reflecting in a ring its cliffs and caverns,
With heaven itself seen like a lake below.

   Compared with this amazing edifice,
Raised by the weakest creatures in existence,
What are the works of intellectual man?

Towers, temples, palaces, and sepulchres;
Ideal images in sculptured forms,
Thoughts hewn in columns or in domes expanded,
Fancies through every maze of beauty shown;
Pride, gratitude, affection, turned to marble
In honor of the living or the dead, —
What are they? fine-wrought miniatures of art,
Too exquisite to bear the weight of dew,
Which every morn lets fall in pearls upon them,
Till all their pomp sinks down in mouldering relics,
Yet in their ruin lovelier than their prime!
Dust in the balance, atoms in the gale,
Compared with these achievements in the deep,
Were all the monuments of olden time,
In days when there were giants on the earth:
Babel's stupendous folly, though it aimed
To scale heaven's battlements, was but a toy,
The plaything of the world in infancy;
The ramparts, towers, and gates of Babylon,
Built for eternity, though, where they stood,
Ruin itself stands still for lack of work,
And Desolation keeps unbroken sabbath, —
Great Babylon, in its full moon of empire,
Even when its " head of gold " was smitten off,
And from a monarch changed into a brute, —
Great Babylon was like a wreath of sand,
Left by one tide and cancelled by the next; —
Egypt's dread wonders, still defying Time,
Where cities have been crumbled into sand,
Scattered by winds beyond the Libyan desert,
Or melted down into the mud of Nile,

And cast in tillage o'er the corn-sown fields,
Where Memphis flourished, and the Pharaohs reigned, —
Egypt's gray piles of hieroglyphic grandeur,
That have survived the language which they speak,
Preserving its dead emblems to the eye,
Yet hiding from the mind what these reveal;
Her pyramids would be mere pinnacles,
Her giant statues, wrought from rocks of granite,
But puny ornaments, for such a pile
As this stupendous mound of catacombs,
Filled with dry mummies of the builder-worms.

      *   *   *

    Nine times the age of man that coral reef
Had bleached beneath the torrid noon, and borne
The thunder of a thousand hurricanes,
Raised by the jealous ocean to repel
That strange encroachment on his old domain.
His rage was impotent; his wrath fulfilled
The counsels of eternal Providence,
And 'stablished what he strove to overturn;
For every tempest threw fresh wrecks upon it;
Sand from the shoals, exuviæ from the deep,
Fragments of shells, dead sloughs, sea-monsters' bones,
Whales stranded in the shallows, hideous weeds
Hurled out of darkness by the uprooting surges,
These, with unutterable relics more,
Heaped the rough surface, till the various mass
By Nature's chemistry combined and purged,
Had buried the bare rock in crumbling mould,
Not unproductive, but from time to time
Impregnated with seeds of plants, and ripe

With embryo animals, or torpid forms
Of reptiles, shrouded in the clefts of trees
From distant lands, with branches, foliage, fruit,
Plucked up and wafted hither by the flood.
Death's spoils and life's hid treasures thus enriched
And colonized the soil; no particle
Of meanest substance but in course was turned
To solid use or noble ornament.
All seasons were propitious; every wind,
From the hot Siroc to the wet Monsoon,
Tempered the crude materials; while heaven's dew
Fell on the sterile wilderness as sweetly
As though it were a garden of the Lord:
Nor fell in vain; each drop had its commission,
And did its duty, known to him who sent it.

Such time had passed, such changes had transfigured
The aspect of that solitary isle,
When I again, in spirit as before,
Assumed mute watch above it. Slender blades
Of grass were shooting through the dark-brown earth,
Like rays of light, transparent in the sun,
Or after showers with liquid gems illumined;
Fountains through filtering sluices sallied forth,
And led fertility where'er they turned;
Green herbage graced their banks, resplendent flowers
Unlocked their treasures, and let flow their fragrance.
Then insect legions, pranked with gaudiest hues,
Pearl, gold, and purple, swarmed into existence;
Minute and marvellous creations these!
Infinite multitudes on every leaf,

In every drop, by me discerned at pleasure, —
Were yet too fine for unenlightened eye,
Like stars, whose beams have never reached our
    world,
Though science meets them midway in the heaven
With prying optics, weighs them in her scale,
Measures their orbs, and calculates their courses; —
Some barely visible, some proudly shone,
Like living jewels; some grotesque, uncouth,
And hideous, — giants of a race of pygmies;
These burrowed in the ground, and fed on garbage;
Those lived deliciously on honey-dews,
And dwelt in palaces of blossomed bells;
Millions on millions, winged, and plumed in front,
And armed with stings for vengeance or assault.
Filled the dim atmosphere with hum and hurry;
Children of light and air and fire they seemed,
Their lives all ecstasy and quick cross-motion.
Thus throve this embryo universe, where all
That was to be was unbegun, or now
Beginning; every day, hour, instant, brought
Its novelty, though how or whence I knew not;
Less than omniscience could not comprehend
The causes of effects that seemed spontaneous,
And sprung in infinite succession, linked
With kindred issues infinite as they.
For which Almighty skill had laid the train
Even in the elements of chaos, whence
The unravelling clew not for a moment lost
Hold of the silent hand that drew it out

      •   •   •

Amphibious monsters haunted the lagoon :
The hippopotamus, amidst the flood
Flexile and active as the smallest swimmer ;
But on the bank, ill-balanced and infirm,
He grazed the herbage, with huge head declined,
Or leaned to rest against some ancient tree :
The crocodile, the dragon of the waters,
In iron panoply, fell as the plague,
And merciless as famine, craunched his prey,
While from his jaws, with dreadful fangs all serried,
The life-blood dyed the waves with deadly streams :
The seal and the sea-lion from the gulf
Came forth, and, crouching with their little ones,
Slept on the shelving rocks that girt the shore,
Securing prompt retreat from sudden danger :
The pregnant turtle, stealing out at eve,
With anxious eye and trembling heart, explored
The loneliest coves, and in the loose, warm sand
Deposited her eggs, which the sun hatched ;
Hence the young brood, that never knew a parent,
Unburrowed, and by instinct sought the sea ;
Nature herself, with her own gentle hand,
Dropping them one by one into the flood,
And laughing to behold their antic joy
When launched in their maternal element.

     *   *   *

High on the cliffs, down on the shelly reef,
Or gliding like a silver-shaded cloud
Through the blue heaven, the mighty albatross
Inhaled the breezes, sought his humble food,
Or, where his kindred like a flock reposed,

Without a shepherd, on the grassy downs,
Smoothed his white fleece, and slumbered in their
    midst.

    Wading through marshes, where the rank sea-weed
With spongy moss and flaccid lichens strove,
Flamingoes, in their crimson tunics, stalked
On stately legs, with far-exploring eye;
Or fed and slept, in regimental lines,
Watched by their sentinels, whose clarion-screams
All in an instant woke the startled troep,
That mounted like a glorious exhalation,
And vanished through the welkin far away,
Nor paused, till, on some lonely coast alighting,
Again their gorgeous cohort took the field.

James Montgomery.

CORAL ISLANDS.

DOWN in the Tropic sea,
    Where the water is warm and deep,
There are gardens fairer than any bee
    Ever saw in its honeyed sleep.

Flowers of crimson bright,
    And green and purple and blue,
In the waters deep which the golden light
    Of the sun sinks softly through.

And many a proud ship sails,
    And many a sea bird flies.

And fishes swim with silvery scales,
  Above where that garden lies.
  *   *   *

You have seen the bright red stem
  Of the wondrous coral tree;
But its living flowers, — you saw not them, —
  They died beneath the sea.

You have seen the coral white,
  The ghastly skeleton;
But the living flowers were a fairer sight
  That used to grow thereon.
  *   *   *

When the lovely flowers are dead,
  And their substance wastes away,
Their skeletons lie on the ocean's bed
  Like wrecks in slow decay.

And over their delicate bones,
  The streams of the lower deep
Lay sand and shell and polished stones
  In many a little heap.
  *   *   *

And this goes on and on,
  And the creatures bloom and grow,
Till the mass of death they rest upon
  Comes upward from below.

And reefs of barren rocks,
  In blue unfathomed seas,
Give rest to the feet of emigrant flocks,
  But have no grass nor trees.

But still the breakers break,
    And white along the shore
The surf leaps high, and the waters make
    Strong barrows as before.

Like barrows made of old
    For ancient British chiefs,
Wherein they lie with torques of gold,
    Are those long coral reefs.

For many a hundred miles
    Those barren reefs extend,
Connecting distant groups of isles
    With paths from end to end.

      *   *   *

And a thousand conscious flowers
    Open their fleshy leaves
To the ocean spray, whose snowy showers
    The thankful mouth receives.

Like the golden mouths that gape
    In the thrush's happy nest,
Open those flowers of starry shape,
    When the sea disturbs their rest.

But when the reef has grown
    Above the highest tide,
It is a city of lifeless stone,
    Whose citizens have died.

For they cannot bear to be
    Where the waters never rise,

And each one, lifted from the sea
  To the parching sunshine, dies.

And bird or wave or wind
  Brings other seeds to sow ;
And on the rock new tenants find
  A soil whereon to grow.

And they have other wants
  Than the flowers the ocean fed ;
The hot sun nurses the living plants,
  And withers up the dead.

And then on the deepening mould
  Of many a hundred years,
When the coral rock is green and old,
  A stunted shrub appears ;

And grasses tall and rank,
  And herbs that thickly teem
Out of the soil on a lake's green bank,
  Or the margin of a stream.

Long ages pass, — those isles
  Have grown maturely fair ;
Green forests wave, and summer smiles,
  And human homes are there.
        *   *   *

Philip Gilbert Hamerton.

THE CORAL INSECT.

TOIL on! toil on! ye ephemeral train,
Who build in the tossing and treacherous main;
Toil on — for the wisdom of man ye mock,
With your sand-based structures and domes of rock;
Your columns the fathomless fountains lave,
And your arches spring up to the crested wave;
Ye're a puny race thus to boldly rear
A fabric so vast in a realm so drear.

Ye bind the deep with your secret zone,
The ocean is sealed, and the surge a stone;
Fresh wreaths from the coral pavement spring,
Like the terraced pride of Assyria's king;
The turf looks green where the breakers rolled;
O'er the whirlpool ripens the rind of gold;
The sea-snatched isle is the home of men,
And mountains exult where the wave hath been.

But why do ye plant 'neath the billows dark
The wrecking reef for the gallant bark?
There are snares enough on the tented field,
Mid the blossomed sweets that the valleys yield;
There are serpents to coil ere the flowers are up;
There's a poison-drop in man's purest cup;
There are foes that watch for his cradle breath,
And why need ye sow the floods with death?

With mouldering bones the deeps are white,
From the ice-clad pole to the tropics bright;

The mermaid hath twisted her fingers cold
With the mesh of the sea-boy's curls of gold,
And the gods of ocean have frowned to see
The mariner's bed in their halls of glee;
Hath earth no graves, that ye thus must spread
The boundless sea for the thronging dead?

Ye build — ye build — but ye enter not in,
Like the tribes whom the desert devoured in their sin;
From the land of promise ye fade and die,
Ere its verdure gleams forth on your weary eye;
As the kings of the cloud-crowned pyramid,
Their noteless bones in oblivion hid,
Ye slumber unmarked mid the desolate main,
While the wonder and pride of your works remain.

Lydia Huntley Sigourney.

THE CORAL GROVE.

DEEP in the wave is a coral grove,
   Where the purple mullet and gold-fish rove;
Where the sea-flower spreads its leaves of blue
That never are wet with falling dew,
But in bright and changeful beauty shine
Far down in the green and glassy brine.
The floor is of sand, like the mountain drift,
And the pearl-shells spangle the flinty snow;
From coral rocks the sea-plants lift
Their boughs, where the tides and billows flow;
The water is calm and still below,

For the winds and waves are absent there,
And the sands are bright as the stars that glow
In the motionless fields of upper air.
There, with its waving blade of green,
The sea-flag streams through the silent water,
And the crimson leaf of the dulse is seen
To blush, like a banner bathed in slaughter.
There, with a light and easy motion,
The fan-coral sweeps through the clear, deep sea,
And the yellow and scarlet tufts of ocean
Are bending like corn on the upland lea.
And life, in rare and beautiful forms,
Is sporting amid those bowers of stone,
And is safe, when the wrathful spirit of storms
Has made the top of the wave his own.
And when the ship from his fury flies,
Where the myriad voices of ocean roar,
When the wind-god frowns in the murky skies,
And demons are waiting the wreck on shore,
Then, far below, in the peaceful sea,
The purple mullet and gold-fish rove
Where the waters murmur tranquilly,
Through the bending twigs of the coral grove.

James Gates Percival

Juan Fernandez.

VERSES

SUPPOSED TO BE WRITTEN BY ALEXANDER SELKIRK DURING
HIS SOLITARY ABODE IN THE ISLAND OF JUAN FER-
NANDEZ.

I AM monarch of all I survey,
   My right there is none to dispute;
From the centre all round to the sea,
   I am lord of the fowl and the brute.
O solitude! where are the charms
   That sages have seen in thy face?
Better dwell in the midst of alarms
   Than reign in this horrible place.

I am out of humanity's reach,
   Must finish my journey alone,
Never hear the sweet music of speech;
   I start at the sound of my own.
The beasts, that roam over the plain,
   My form with indifference see;
They are so unacquainted with man,
   Their tameness is shocking to me.

Society, friendship, and love,
   Divinely bestowed upon man,
O, had I the wings of a dove,
   How soon would I taste you again!

My sorrows I then might assuage
   In the ways of religion and truth,
Might learn from the wisdom of age,
   And be cheered by the sallies of youth.

Religion! what treasure untold
   Resides in that heavenly word!
More precious than silver and gold,
· Or all that this earth can afford.
But the sound of the church-going bell
   These valleys and rocks never heard,
Never sighed at the sound of a knell,
   Or smiled when a sabbath appeared.

Ye winds that have made me your sport,
   Convey to this desolate shore
Some cordial endearing report
   Of a land I shall visit no more.
My friends, do they now and then send
   A wish or a thought after me?
O, tell me I yet have a friend,
   Though a friend I am never to see.

How fleet is a glance of the mind!
   Compared with the speed of its flight,
The tempest itself lags behind,
   And the swift-winged arrows of light.
When I think of my own native land,
   In a moment I seem to be there;
But alas! recollection at hand
   Soon hurries me back to despair.

But the sea-fowl is gone to her nest,
    The beast has laid down in his lair;
Even here is a season of rest,
    And I to my cabin repair.
There 's mercy in every place,
    And mercy, encouraging thought!
Gives even affliction a grace,
    And reconciles man to his lot.

William Cowper.

Madeira.

MADEIRA.

THEN Macham, who (through love to long adventures
      led)
Medera's wealthy Isles the first discovered,
Who having stolen a maid, to whom he was affied,
Yet her rich parents still her marriage rites denied,
Put with her forth to sea, where, many a danger past,
Upon an isle of those at length by tempest cast;
And putting in, to give his tender love some ease,
Which very ill had brooked the rough and boisterous
      seas;
And lingering for her health within the quiet bay,
The mariners most false fled with the ship away,
When as it was not long but she gave up her breath;
When he whose tears in vain bewailed her timeless
      death,

That their deservéd rites her funeral could not have,
A homely altar built upon her honored grave.
When with his folk but few, not passing two or three,
There making them a boat, but rudely of one tree,
Put forth again to sea, where after many a flaw,
Such as before themselves scarce mortal ever saw,
Nor miserable men could possibly sustain,
Now swallowed with the waves, and then spewed up
    again,
At length were on the coast of sunburnt Affrick
    thrown,
T' amaze that further world, and to amuse our own.

                      Michael Drayton.

MADEIRA.

THE favoring gales invite; the bowsprit bears
    Right onward to the fearful shade; more black
The cloudy spectre towers; already fear
Shrinks at the view aghast and breathless. Hark!
'T was more than the deep murmur of the surge
That struck the ear; whilst through the lurid gloom
Gigantic phantoms seem to lift in air
Their misty arms; yet, yet, · bear boldly on, —
The mist dissolves; seen through the parting haze,
Romantic rocks, like the depictured clouds,
Shine out; beneath, a blooming wilderness
Of varied wood is spread, that scents the air;
Where fruits of "golden rind," thick interspersed
And pendent, through the mantling umbrage gleam

Inviting. Cypress here, and stateliest pine,
Spire o'er the nether shades, as emulous
Of sole distinction where all nature smiles.
Some trees, in sunny glades alone their head
And graceful stem uplifting, mark below
The turf with shadow; whilst in rich festoons
The flowery lianes braid their boughs; meantime
Choirs of innumerous birds of liveliest song
And brightest plumage, flitting through the shades,
With nimble glance are seen; they, unalarmed,
Now near in airy circles sing, then speed
Their random flight back to their sheltering bowers,
Whose silence, broken only by their song,
From the foundation of this busy world,
Perhaps had never echoed to the voice,
Or heard the steps of Man. What rapture fired
The strangers' bosoms, as from glade to glade
They passed, admiring all, and gazing still
With new delight! 'T is solitude around;
Deep solitude, that on the gloom of woods
Primeval fearful hangs: a green recess
Now opens in the wilderness; gay flowers
Of unknown name purple the yielding sward;
The ring-dove murmurs o'er their head, like one
Attesting tenderest joy; but mark the trees,
Where, slanting through the gloom, the sunshine rests!
Beneath, a moss-grown monument appears,
O'er which the green banana gently waves
Its long leaf; and an aged cypress near
Leans, as if listening to the streamlet's sound
That gushes from the adverse bank; but pause, —

Approach with reverence ! Maker of the world,
There is a Christian's cross ! and on the stone
A name, yet legible amid its moss, —
Anna !

William Lisle Bowles.

INSCRIPTION FOR THE GRAVE OF ANNA D'ARFET.

O'ER my poor Anna's lowly grave
    No dirge shall sound, no knell shall ring ;
But angels. as the high pines wave,
    Their half-heard " Miserere " sing.

No flowers of transient bloom at eve
    The maidens on the turf shall strew ;
Nor sigh, as the sad spot they leave,
    Sweets to the sweet ! a long adieu !

But in this wilderness profound,
    O'er her the dove shall build her nest ;
And ocean swell with softer sound
    A requiem to her dreams of rest !

Ah ! when shall I as quiet be,
    When not a friend, or human eye,
Shall mark beneath the mossy tree
    The spot where we forgotten lie ?

To kiss her name on the cold stone
    Is all that now on earth I crave ;
For in this world I am alone, —
    O, lay me with her in the grave !

Robert à Machin.   Tr. W. L. Bowles.

THE ISLAND OF MADEIRA.

THOUGH never axe until a later day
  Assailed thy forests' huge antiquity,
Yet elder Fame had many tales of thee, —
Whether Phœnician shipman far astray
Had brought uncertain notices away
Of islands dreaming in the middle sea;
Or that man's heart, which struggles to be free
From the old worn-out world, had never stay
Till, for a place to rest on, it had found
A region out of ken, -- that happier isle,
Which the mild ocean-breezes blow around, —
Where they who thrice upon this mortal stage
Had kept their hands from wrong, their hearts from
      guile,
Should come at length, and live a tearless age.
                              Richard Chenevix Trench.

Malta.

ODE TO THE LIGHTHOUSE AT MALTA.

THE world in dreary darkness sleeps profound, —
  The storm-clouds hurry on, by hoarse winds driven,
And night's dull shades and spectral mists confound
  Earth, sea, and heaven!

King of surrounding chaos! thy dim form
  Rises with fiery crown upon thy brow,
To scatter light and peace amid the storm,
  And life bestow.

In vain the sea with thundering waves may peal
  And burst beneath thy feet in giant sport,
Till the white foam in snowy clouds conceal
  The sheltering port.

Thy flaming tongue proclaims — "Behold the shore!"
  And voiceless hails the weary pilot back,
Whose watchful eyes, like worshippers, explore
  Thy shining track.

Now silent night a gorgeous mantle wears,
  By sportive winds the clouds are scattered far,
And lo! with starry train the moon appears
  In circling car.

While the pale mist that thy tall brow enshrouds
  In vain would veil thy diadem from sight,
Whose form colossal seems to touch the clouds
  With starlike light.

Ocean's perfidious waves may calmly sleep,
  Yet hide sharp rocks — the cliff false signs display:
And luring lights, far flashing o'er the deep,
  The ship betray.

But thou, whose splendor dims each lesser beam,
  Whose firm, unmoved position might declare

Thy throne a monarch's — like the north-star's gleam,
   Reveals each snare.

So Reason's steady torch, with light as pure,
   Dispels the gloom when stormy passions rise,
Or Fortune's cheating phantoms would obscure
   The soul's dim eyes!

Since I am cast by adverse fortunes here,
   Where thou presidest o'er this scanty soil,
And bounteous heaven a shelter grants to cheer
   My spirit's toil;

Frequent I turn to thee, with homage mute,
   Ere yet each troubled thought is calmed in sleep,
And still thy gem-like brow my eyes salute
   Above the deep.

How many now may gaze on this sea-shore,
   Alas! like me, as exiles doomed to roam!
Some who perchance would greet a wife once more,
   Or children's home;

Wanderers, by poverty or despots driven
   To seek a refuge, as I do, afar,
Here find, at last, the sign of welcome given, —
   A hospitable star!

And still to guide the barque it calmly shines, —
   The barque that from my native land oft bears
Tidings of bitter griefs, and mournful lines
   Written with tears.

When first thy vision flashed upon my eyes,
  And all its dazzling glory I beheld,
Oh, how my heart, long used to miseries,
  With rapture swelled!

Inhospitable Latium's shores were lost,
  And, as amid the threatening waves we steered,
When near to dangerous shoals, by tempests tost,
  Thy light appeared.

No saints the fickle mariners then praised,
  But vows and prayers forgot they with the night;
While from the silent gloom the cry was raised, —
  "Malta in sight!"

And thou wert like a sainted image crowned,
  Whose forehead bears a shower of golden rays,
Which pilgrims, seeking health and peace, surround
  With holy praise.

Never may I forget thee! One alone
  Of cherished objects shall with thee aspire,
King of the night! to match thy lofty throne
  And friendly fire.

That vision still with sparkling light appears
  In the sun's dazzling beams at matin hour,
And is the golden angel memory rears
  On Cordova's proud tower!

El Duque de Rivas. Tr. Anon.

THE KNIGHTS OF ST. JOHN.

OH, nobly shone the fearful cross upon your mail afar,
　When Rhodes and Acre hailed your might, O lions
　　of the war!
When leading many a pilgrim horde, through wastes
　of Syrian gloom;　　　　　　·
Or standing with the cherub's sword before the Holy
　Tomb.
Yet on your forms the apron seemed a nobler armor
　far,
When by the sick man's bed ye stood, O lions of the
　war!
When ye, the high-born, bowed your pride to tend the
　lowly weakness,
The duty, though it brought no fame, fulfilled by Chris-
　tian meekness, —
Religion of the cross, thou blend'st, as in a single flower,
The twofold branches of the palm, — humility and power.

Friedrich von Schiller.　Tr. Edward, Lord Lytton.

St. Helena.

ON THE DEATH OF NAPOLEON.

HE was: and motionless in death,
　As that unconscious clay,
Robbed of so mighty breath,
In speechless ruin lay,

Even so, bewildered, stunned, aghast,
    Earth at the tale is dumb,
Pondering the final agonies
Of him, the man of fate,
And wondering when, with tread like his,
Again to desolate
Her trampled fields, all dust and blood,
    A mortal foot shall come.

Him, upon his refulgent throne,
In silence could my soul survey,
And when, by varying fortunes blown,
He fell, rose — fell again and lay,
My spirit to the millions' tone
    Echoed back no reply;
Virgin alike from servile praise
And cowardly abuse;
But now, as wane the meteor's rays,
I let my genius loose,
To fall upon his urn one strain
    Perchance that shall not die.

From the Alps to the Pyramids,
From the Manzanar to the Rhine,
He tracked his eagles, as the bolt
Follows its flashing sign.
From Tanais to Scylla glancing,
    From the West to the Eastern brine;
Was this true greatness? — That high doom
Let after times declare;
We to the Greatest bow, from whom

He held so large a share
Of the Most High, creative mind,
　　Stamped by the hand divine.

The tremulous, tempestuous joy
Of lofty enterprise — the heart
That knew no rest from its employ,
But burned to play the imperial part;
And won and kept a prize whose dream
　　Had madness seemed, at best —
All he had proved and passed — renown
That after danger brightest smiled,
Defeat and flight, and victory's crown,
A ruler now, and now exiled, —
Twice humbled in the dust, defiled,
　　Twice at the altar blest.

Two ages, 'gainst each other armed,
Him for their umpire named,
Looking on him as Fate: he charmed
To silence their contentions — tamed
Their frantic feuds, and sat supreme
　　Their factious rage above:
He vanished — and his vacant days
Spent in so small a sphere!
Majestic mark for envy's gaze,
And pity most sincere —
For unextinguishable hate,
　　And never-vanquished love.

As on the shipwrecked seaman's head
The o'erwhelming breakers pour,

Beyond whose foaming fury spread
Around him and before,
The wretch had vainly gazed to see
  The intangible, far strand;
Thus o'er that strong but sinking soul
Swept Memory's whelming tide,
As oft his actions to enroll
In Fame's recórds he tried; —
But from the everlasting scroll
  Fell, faint, his harassed hand.

O, at the silent, dying hour
Of some dull day of rest,
His lightning eyes in sullen lower,
And his arms folded on his breast,
How often have his days of power
  Rushed on remembrance thick!
Then to his backward-roving thought
The moving tents, the trench, the course,
The gleaming squadrons have been brought,
The sea-like surging of the horse,
The martial word, the swift command,
  The obedience, no less quick.

Alas! at such an overthrow
Haply that panting spirit failed;
Haply despairing drooped: but, lo!
The Omnipotent from heaven hailed
His child, and unto purer air,
  With pitying hand conveyed;
And through the flowery paths of hope

Dismissed him to the eternal fields,
Where more than even his lofty scope
Perfect fruition yields,
And where the glory that hath past
    Is silence now, and shade.

Beneficent, immortal, fair,
Faith holds her wonted triumph yet:
Write this besides: Rejoice! for ne'er
Did haughtier potentate forget
His pride, and meekly bow at last,
    To Golgotha's disgrace.
Thou, o'er his weary dust, each low
Calumnious word forbear;
The God from whom afflictions flow,
All comfort and all care,
Beside him deigned, on his low bed,
    To find a resting-place.

        Alessandro Manzoni.   Tr. T. W. Parsons.

PASSING ST. HELENA.

AND this is St. Helena? This the spot
  Haunted forever by an Emperor!
Methinks 't were meet that such a royal ghost
Should pace these gloomy battlements by night!
—— The ship veered off, and we passed out to sea:
And in the first fair moonrise of the month,
I watched the island, till it seemed a speck
No bigger than Astarte.   Year by year,

The picture came and went upon my brain,
Like frost-work on the windows : in my dreams
I saw those jagged turrets of dull rock
Uplifted in the moonlight ; saw the gulls
Darting in sudden circles ; heard the low
And everlasting anthem of the sea !
And from the nether world a voice would come,
Here did they bring the Corsican, and here
Died the chained eagle by these dismal cliffs !

Thomas Bailey Aldrich.

NAPOLEON AT REST.

HIS falchion flashed along the Nile,
  His host he led through Alpine snows,
O'er Moscow's towers, that blazed the while,
  His eagle-flag unrolled — and froze !

Here sleeps he now, alone ! — not one,
  Of all the kings whose crowns he gave
Bends o'er his dust ; nor wife nor son
  Has ever seen or sought his grave.

Behind the sea-girt rock the star
  That led him on from crown to crown
Has sunk, and nations from afar
  Gazed as it faded and went down.

High is his tomb : the ocean flood,
  Far, far below, by storms is curled, —
As round him heaved, while high he stood,
  A stormy and unstable world.

Alone he sleeps : the mountain cloud,
　　That night hangs round him, and the breath
Of morning scatters, is the shroud
　　That wraps the conqueror's clay in death.

Pause here !　The far-off world at last
　　Breathes free ; the hand that shook its thrones,
And to the earth its mitres cast,
　　Lies powerless now beneath these stones.

Hark !　Comes there from the pyramids,
　　And from Siberian wastes of snow,
And Europe's hills, a voice that bids
　　The world be awed to mourn him ? — No !

The only, the perpetual dirge
　　That 's heard here, is the sea-bird's cry, —
The mournful murmur of the surge,
　　The cloud's deep voice, the wind's low sigh.

　　　　　　　　　　　　John Pierpont.

THE PHANTOM SHIP.

THE clouds are dark, and the winds are wailing ;
　　The sky is deserted of moon and star.
It is the hour when the ship goeth sailing
　　Along the dusk ocean fast and far.
That lone ship, steered by a viewless hand,
　　And pauseless on her path,
No storm shall wreck ; she shall reach the strand
　　Unharmed by the elements' wrath.

Far out in the offing, where on the billows
  The winds are dumb, and the stilled air dies,
Arises a barren rock, and pillows
  Its naked head amid burning skies.
There nothing bloometh of green or soft;
  No blithe bird nestles there;
The eagle alone, from his throne aloft,
  Reigns over a desert bare.

Yet there sleeps he who was Europe's lord,
  Her king, her hero, her man of doom,
And his head-gear, golden sceptre, and sword
  Lie noteless on his forsaken tomb.
No voice bewails the illustrious dead;
  It is silentness all and dearth,
It is ghastly gloom round the last low bed
  Of the mightiest spirit of earth!

And the moons roll round, and the seasons duly,
  And stark the emperor lieth alway,
Till again in its course refalleth newly
  The stormful night of the fifth of May.
Amiddle that black and dolorous night
  He passed from this world of strife,
And, when it returns, in the swift year's flight,
  He awakes for a while to life.

And now, as the conquered gale is dying,
  The ship approaches in phantom-show,
A spectre-flag at her mast-head flying
  Of golden bees on a field of snow.

And the king embarks, in the moonlight blue,
   And away she hies as a bird,
Without a pilot, without a crew,
   And with sails all wind-unstirred.

He paces her deck, that hero of story,
   And looks abroad through the desert night.
His thoughts fly back to his years of glory;
   His eyes rekindle with living light.
And on she speeds to the ancient shore
   Of history and romance, —
And the hero's heart leaps up once more, —
   He knows his beloved France!

Again he treadeth her soil, which trembles
   Beneath the feet of the genius of war;
But, how changed seems all! The land resembles
   The wreck, the shell of a burnt-out star!
He seeketh her cities, but findeth none, —
   He looks for her armies in vain, —
They flourished, they lived, but under the sun
   Of his resplendent reign!

He seeks the throne that he won by conquest;
   'T is trod into dust with the things that were.
France knows it no more! Yet still hath he one
      quest, —
   The father looks round for his royal heir;
He calls aloud for the boy whose birth
   Was hailed as the hope of the age;
Alas! his life is outblotted from earth,
   His name from history's page!

"All, all are gone!" cries the desolate-hearted, —
  "My glory, my people, my son, my crown!
O, how are the days of my power departed!
  How lost is the nation I raised to renown!
My house and my hopes alike lie prone
  In an all-engulfing grave, —
A slave sits now upon Cæsar's throne,
  And Cæsar hath sunk to a slave!"

                  From the German. Tr. Anon.

THE EXHUMATION OF NAPOLEON.

FIT tomb was St. Helena, O Napoleon, for thee!
  A barren rock, that far and lone was planted in
    the sea!
The wild untainted sea-gales there could sigh above
  thy turf,
And thy requiem was the moaning of the ever-plung-
  ing surf;
No busy jar of restless life, no hurrying feet were near,
There came the watchful stars alone, and the revolv-
  ing year; —
The scourge and dread of Europe, whose cannons'
  conquering roar
Pealed down the towering Pyrenees and rang from
  shore to shore,
Whose restless and impatient heart in life could find
  no room,
Had the ocean for a mourner, and an island for a
  tomb.

Thy lifeless body they exhumed, when thou wast but
 a name,
When thy tongue was still as silence, and thy ear was
 deaf to fame :
The exiled corpse, that could not harm, they lifted from
 the grave,
And in solemn triumph bore it to its home across the
 wave ;
Mid the shriek and wail of trumpets, in long and solemn train,
In thy funeral car they bore thee to thy grave beside
 the Seine.
And thou whose first return had been in triumph and
 in pride,
When the glad acclaim of thousands was pealing far
 and wide,
When the warrior crowned with laurels came a throne
 to reassume,
Came back at last, a silent corpse, to crumble in a tomb.

They laid thee, while the trifling world forgot the
 song and dance,
In a splendid mausoleum in the populous heart of
 France ;
The costly mockery of woe with the pageant passed
 away,
And thou, dead conqueror, couldst win from pleasure
 but a day ;
Through all the city's arteries again in toil and strife
Whirled on with eddying current the hurrying tide of
 life ;

The busy hum of Paris was dinning o'er thy head,
And the reckless passer hurried by and thought not of
    the dead, —
The pomp and pageantry were past, the burial was o'er,
And Napoleon slept as lonely there as on Helena's
    shore.

William Wetmore Story.

North Pole.

PRAYER AT THE POLE.

A LITTLE group of worn-out men,
　With weary limbs and shattered forms,
Whose stalwart wills and gallant hearts
　Were strong to face dark danger's storms!
And one amidst them, slight of frame,
　And pale from strife with death and pain,
A hero's soul, whose martyr zeal
　Bore nobly suffering's cankering chain!

They met within the solemn aisles
　Of ice-built shrine, a temple grand,
Alone upon a frozen sea,
　The saving and the rescued band,
Mid crystal columns reared aloft
　Against a gray and cloud-draped dome, —
The only thing — that shadowed sky —
　In all the waste that looked like home!

They stood with bowed, uncovered heads,
　With reverent mien and moistened eyes,

Remembering scenes that long had passed,
  Recalling love's most tender ties,
As softly on the keen, cold air
  Their leader's voice rose calm and clear,
And raised, like prophet's tone, the hope
  That in each heart had found a bier.

Few words of humble, grateful praise,
  For guidance, life, and rest, a prayer,
A low "Amen" from quivering lips,
  Were all the pomps of service there!
It gave them strength to conquer death;
  It made them brave to dare and do;
It kept them faithful to the end,
  A band of brothers, tried and true!

Then bless them, souls of Christian men
  O'er all the earth who praise and pray;
And bless him most of all, their chief,
  Who first in duty led the way, —
Who first upon those regions drear
  Of frozen, unknown waters spoke
The name of Christ, whose world-blessed sound
  The solitude of silence broke!

Those polar mounts of ice may melt
  Beneath the Arctic's summer skies;
May speed the nations' hoarded wealth,
  And 'neath the tropics ebb and rise;
Yet bear abroad, where'er they flow,
  That baptism of the holy Name
They echoed from his voice who died
  And left those bergs to spread his fame!

                                   Sallie Bridges.

Polar Regions.

A SCENE IN THE POLAR REGIONS.

FAR in the north, behind the Oreades,
   The setting sun a twilight glimmer shed;
Eastward afar the coasts of men were seen
Dim, shadowy, and spectral; like a still,
Broad land of spirits lay the vacant sea
Beneath the empty heavens; — here and there
Perchance a vessel skimmed the watery waste,
Like a white-winged sea-bird; but it moved
Too pale and small beneath the veil of space.
Sublime and awful solitude! the heart,
As it broods over thee, beats fast, and feels
Ennobled! — Thou, too, goest forth, pale sun;
Like a white angel, goest down to visit
The silent, ice-walled cloister of the pole,
And, drawing after thee thy bridal garment,
That floats in gold upon the weltering wave,
Veilest thyself around! Where art thou now,
Pale one in rosy robes? Wilt glimmer forth
Again into a warm and glowing eye
Among the ice-fields? — Standing here, I gaze
Down on the dreary winter of the world.
How dumb and endless is it down below!
The almighty, outstretched giant stirs himself
In all his thousand limbs, and wrinkles up,
And nothing remains great before him, save

His Father, the great Heaven!—Mighty Son!
Wilt lead me to the Father, when, at last,
I come to thee?—-
    Lo, what a gorgeous spectacle! Aurora
Upon the ruddy evening twilight glows,
With fast increasing light. What can it be
That rends away so suddenly the dark
Shroud of the watery Orcus? How the shores
Of men like golden morning blaze! Oh, art thou
Already come to us again, thou fair,
Majestic Sun, so young and rosy-red?
And wilt thou journey kindly yet once more
A long day's journey o'er the fields of men?—
Glow upward, then, immortal one!—I stand
Yet cold and pale on my horizon: soon
I must go down to the dark realms of ice.
But shall I, too, like him, O God, arise
More warm and bright again, to journey through
A long, bright day in thy eternity?
        Jean Paul Richter. Versified by C. T. Brooks.

THE ARCTIC VOYAGER.

SHALL I desist, twice baffled? Once by land,
And once by sea, I fought and strove with storms.
All shades of danger, tides, and weary calms;
Head-currents, cold and famine, savage beasts,
And men more savage; all the while my face
Looked northward toward the pole; if mortal strength
Could have sustained me, I had never turned

Till I had seen the star which never sets
Freeze in the Arctic zenith. That I failed
To solve the mysteries of the ice-bound world,
Was not because I faltered in the quest.
Witness those pathless forests which conceal
The bones of perished comrades, that long march,
Blood-tracked o'er flint and snow, and one dread night
By Athabasca, when a cherished life
Flowed to give life to others. This, and worse,
I suffered — let it pass — it has not tamed
My spirit nor the faith which was my strength.
Despite of waning years, despite the world
Which doubts, the few who dare, I purpose now —
A purpose long and thoughtfully resolved,
Through all its grounds of reasonable hope —
To seek beyond the ice which guards the Pole
A sea of open water; for I hold,
Not without proofs, that such a sea exists,
And may be reached, though since this earth was made
No keel hath ploughed it, and to mortal ear
No wind hath told its secrets. . . . . With this tide
I sail; if all be well, this very moon
Shall see my ship beyond the southern cape
Of Greenland, and far up the bay through which,
With diamond spire and gorgeous pinnacle,
The fleets of winter pass to warmer seas.
Whether, my hardy shipmates! we shall reach
Our bourn, and come with tales of wonder back,
Or whether we shall lose the precious time,
Locked in thick ice, or whether some strange fate
Shall end us all, I know not; but I know

A lofty hope, if earnestly pursued,
Is its own crown, and never in this life
Is labor wholly fruitless. In this faith
I shall not count the chances, — sure that all
A prudent foresight asks we shall not want,
And all that bold and patient hearts can do
Ye will not leave undone. The rest is God's !

Henry Timrod.

HYMN TO THE NORTH STAR.

THE sad and solemn night
  Has yet her multitude of cheerful fires ;
The glorious host of light
Walk the dark hemisphere till she retires ;
All through her silent watchings, gliding slow,
Her constellations come, and climb the heavens, and go.

Day, too, hath many a star
To grace his gorgeous reign, as bright as they :
  Through the blue fields afar,
Unseen, they follow in his flaming way :
Many a bright lingerer, as the eve grows dim,
Tells what a radiant troop arose and set with him.

And thou dost see them rise,
Star of the Pole ! and thou dost see them set.
  Alone, in thy cold skies,
Thou keep'st thy old unmoving station yet,
Nor join'st the dances of that glittering train,
Nor dipp'st thy virgin orb in the blue western main.

There, at morn's rosy birth,
Thou lookest meekly through the kindling air;
    And eve, that round the earth
Chases the day, beholds thee watching there;
There noontide finds thee, and the hour that calls
The shapes of polar flame to scale heaven's azure walls.

    Alike, beneath thine eye,
The deeds of darkness and of light are done;
    High towards the star-lit sky
Towns blaze, — the smoke of battle blots the sun, —
The night-storm on a thousand hills is loud, —
And the strong wind of day doth mingle sea and cloud.

    On thy unaltering blaze
The half-wrecked mariner, his compass lost,
    Fixes his steady gaze,
And steers, undoubting, to the friendly coast;
And they who stray in perilous wastes, by night,
Are glad when thou dost shine, to guide their footsteps
    right.

    And, therefore, bards of old,
Sages, and hermits of the solemn wood,
    Did in thy beams behold
A beauteous type of that unchanging Good,
That bright eternal Beacon, by whose ray
The voyager of time should shape his heedful way.

                    William Cullen Bryant.

THE FLAMINGO.

THE red flamingo flew up from the South,
From the land all withered and parched with drouth.

He gleamed on the sky like a flaming brand
Blown from a burning prairie land.

He waded deep through the dark morass,
In the samphire beds, and the cool dank grass.

When the wind blew east, to the sea he went,
Red as the sun in the firmament,

And turned aside, with a look aslant,
At the deadly eye of the cormorant.

And the eagle, old with a hundred years,
From the height of his vaulted eyry peers.

When the wind blew west, to the fields he sped,
Where the blue-eyed gentian lifts its head;

And the dew flushed red to a scarlet dye
On the lily's breast, as he floated by;

And here and there, in the silent dell,
From his wing a scarlet feather fell.

He sailed on his way as the mariner sails,
With stout heart fearing nor wind nor gales.

On and on through the land he went,
Like a fleet and royal messenger sent,

Till he came at last to an ancient town
Never on map or chart laid down.

His wearied wings beat soft and low,
For the dreary streets were of muffled snow.

The houses were counted by two and two,
And the footsteps numbered were faint and few.

The ships that had sailed to that silent shore
Were bound, snow-locked, without mast or oar.

The shrouds had vanished, — a dreary wreck,
With the tropic bird on the lonely deck.

His eye grew dim in the cold, wan light,
And his royal plumage blanched snow-white.

He strained his gaze to the farthest north,
And again on fluttering wings went forth,

And sailed away, with his plumage pale
Forever hid by a snowy veil.

Whether he drifted east or west,
And gazed on a mighty mountain crest,

Or a glorious sea with turrets high
Reaching far up to the polar sky,

Or drooped in death on a waste of snow,
His secret none shall ever know.

He lived his life on his errand sent,
And tracked the path of a continent.

Whoever has crossed to that silent strand
Has passed beyond to an unknown land.

Buried in snow, and under the gates,
Frozen and stark the sentinel waits

Till the snow shall be lifted from off his breast,
And the pathway cleared to the great Northwest!

Sarah D. Clarke.

THE ARCTIC OCEAN.

A WEIRD and awful sea, its surges roll
   In solitude, and unexplored expand
From age to age around the Arctic pole,
   And beat with hollow roar a frozen land,
Whose adamantine crags behold no sail
Reel on that howling ocean to the northern gale.

No ancient capitals its shores adorn,
   With domes and pinnacles glancing royal gold;
But on its wonderful, untrodden bourn
   Rise battlements of ice, whose turrets, old
As the creation's dawn, forever gleam
Like orient pearl beneath the North's auroral beam.

No treasures delved by slaves in cavern gloom
   Lie buried underneath its hoary wave;
Its wildest tempests never knolled the doom
   Of wretches sinking to a watery grave.
Resounds not there the combat's baleful trump,
Nor battle smoke enshrouds its midnight's starry pomp.

The same as when the choral stars sang forth
　Their jubilee throughout the eternal arc,
Still heaves the desolate ocean of the North;
　Still o'er its waters broods primeval dark,
Mysterious twilight throbbing with the chime
Of constellations ringing out the march of Time.

Perchance the hero of the British isle,
　Much wept, much sought for, slumbers on that coast,
His faithful comrades by his side; the while
　For noble hearts that perished at their post
The dreary winds sweep o'er the angry surge,
And with a melancholy music chant their dirge.

Ay, what a sepulchre for hero's head!
　The stars, undying links, light up his tomb,
Majestic bergs, like angels, watch the dead,
　And ever upwards through the polar gloom
Most solemn and sublime the wild wind rolls
The grand cathedral hymn for the departed souls.

Seymour Green Wheeler Benjamin.

NORTHERN SEAS.

UP! up! let us a voyage take;
　Why sit we here at ease?
Find us a vessel tight and snug,
Bound for the Northern Seas.

I long to see the Northern Lights,
With their rushing splendors, fly

Like living things, with flaming wings,
Wide o'er the wondrous sky.

I long to see those icebergs vast,
With heads all crowned with snow,
Whose green roots sleep in the awful deep,
Two hundred fathoms low.

I long to hear the thundering crash
Of their terrific fall;
And the echoes from a thousand cliffs
Like lovely voices call.

There shall we see the fierce white bear;
The sleepy seals aground;
And the spouting whales, that to and fro
Sail with a dreary sound.

There may we tread on depths of ice,
That the hairy mammoth hide;
Perfect as when, in times of old,
The mighty creature died.

And whilst the unsetting sun shines on
Through the still heaven's deep blue,
We'll traverse the azure waves, the herds
Of the dread sea-horse to view.

We'll pass the shore of solemn pine,
Where wolves and black bears prowl;
And away to the rocky isles of mist,
To rouse the northern fowl.

Up there shall start ten thousand wings,
With a rushing, whistling din;
Up shall the auk and fulmar start, —
All but the fat penguin.

And there, in the wastes of the silent sky,
With the silent earth below,
We shall see, far off to his lonely rock,
The lonely eagle go.

Then softly, softly will we tread
By inland streams, to see
Where the pelican of the silent north
Sits there all silently.

But if thou love the Southern Seas,
And pleasant summer weather,
Come, let us mount this gallant ship,
And sail away together.

William Howitt.

ON THE ICE ISLANDS,

SEEN FLOATING IN THE GERMAN OCEAN.

WHAT portents, from that distant region, ride,
Unseen till now in ours, the astonished tide?
In ages past, old Proteus, with his droves
Of sea-calves, sought the mountains and the groves.
But now descending whence of late they stood,
Themselves the mountains seem to rove the flood.
Dire times were they, full-charged with human woes;

And these, scarce less calamitous than those.
What view we now? More wondrous still? Behold!
Like burnished brass they shine, or beaten gold;
And all around the pearl's pure splendor show,
And all around the ruby's fiery glow.
Come they from India, where the burning earth,
All bounteous, gives her richest treasures birth;
And where the costly gems, that beam around
The brows of mightiest potentates, are found?
No. Never such a countless dazzling store
Had left, unseen, the Ganges' peopled shore.
Rapacious hands, and ever-watchful eyes,
Should sooner far have marked and seized the prize.
Whence sprang they then? Ejected have they come
From Ves'vius' or from Ætna's burning womb!
Thus shine they self-illumed, or but display
The borrowed splendors of a cloudless day?
With borrowed beams they shine. The gales, that
          breathe
Now landward, and the current's force beneath,
Have borne them nearer: and the nearer sight,
Advantaged more, contemplates them aright.
Their lofty summits crested high, they show,
With mingled sleet, and long incumbent snow.
The rest is ice. Far hence, where most severe
Bleak winter wellnigh saddens all the year,
Their infant growth began He bade arise
Their uncouth forms, portentous in our eyes
Oft as dissolved by transient suns, the snow
Left the tall cliff, to join the flood below;
He caught, and curdled with a freezing blast

The current ere it reached the boundless waste.
By slow degrees uprose the wondrous pile,
And long successive ages rolled the while;
Till, ceaseless in its growth, it claimed to stand,
Tall as its rival mountains on the land.
Thus stood, and unremovable by skill,
Or force of man, had stood the structure still;
But that, though firmly fixed, supplanted yet
By pressure of its own enormous weight,
It left the shelving beach, and with a sound
That shook the bellowing waves and rocks around
Self-launched, and swiftly, to the briny wave,
As if instinct with strong desire to lave,
Down went the ponderous mass. So bards of old,
How Delos swam the Ægean deep, have told.
But not of ice was Delos. Delos bore
Herb, fruit, and flower. She, crowned with laurel, wore,
Even under wintry skies, a summer smile;
And Delos was Apollo's favorite isle.
But, horrid wanderers of the deep, to you
He deems Cimmerian darkness only due.
Your hated birth he deigned not to survey,
But, scornful, turned his glorious eyes away.
Hence! seek your home, no longer rashly dare
The darts of Phœbus, and a softer air;
Lest ye regret, too late, your native coast,
In no congenial gulf forever lost!

                                     William Cowper.

THE ARCTIC LOVER.

GONE is the long, long winter night;
  Look, my beloved one!
How glorious, through his depths of light,
  Rolls the majestic sun!
The willows, waked from winter's death,
Give out a fragrance like thy breath, —
  The summer is begun!

Ay, 't is the long bright summer day:
  Hark, to that mighty crash!
The loosened ice-ridge breaks away,
  The smitten waters flash.
Seaward the glittering mountain rides,
While down its green translucent sides
  The foamy torrents dash.

See, love, my boat is moored for thee,
  By ocean's weedy floor, -
The petrel does not skim the sea
  More swiftly than my oar.
We 'll go where, on the rocky isles,
Her eggs the screaming sea-fowl piles
  Beside the pebbly shore.

Or, bide thou where the poppy blows,
  With wind-flowers frail and fair,
While I, upon his isle of snows,
  Seek and defy the bear.
Fierce though he be, and huge of frame,

This arm his savage strength shall tame,
   And drag him from his lair.

When crimson sky and flamy cloud
   Bespeak the summer o'er,
And the dead valleys wear a shroud
   Of snows that melt no more,
I 'll build of ice thy winter home,
With glistening walls and glassy dome,
   And spread with skins the floor.

The white fox by thy couch shall play;
   And from the frozen skies
The meteors of a mimic day
   Shall flash upon thine eyes.
And I — for such thy vow — meanwhile
Shall hear thy voice and see thy smile,
   Till that long midnight flies.

               William Cullen Bryant.

ICE-BLINK.

'T IS sunset : to the firmament serene
  The Atlantic wave reflects a gorgeous scene;
Broad in the cloudless west a belt of gold
Girds the blue hemisphere; above, unrolled,
The keen clear air grows palpable to sight,
Embodied in a flush of crimson light,
Through which the evening star, with milder gleam,
Descends, to meet her image in the stream.
Far in the east, what spectacle unknown
Allures the eye to gaze on it alone?

Amidst black rocks, that lift on either hand
Their countless peaks, and mark receding land;
Amidst a tortuous labyrinth of seas,
That shine around the arctic Cyclades;
Amidst a coast of dreariest continent,
In many a shapeless promontory rent;
O'er rocks, seas, islands, promontories spread,
The Ice-Blink rears its undulated head,
On which the sun, beyond the horizon shrined,
Hath left his richest garniture behind;
Piled on a hundred arches, ridge by ridge,
O'er fixed and fluid, strides the Alpine bridge,
Whose blocks of sapphire seem to mortal eye
Hewn from cerulean quarries of the sky;
With glacier-battlements, that crowd the spheres,
The slow creation of six thousand years,
Amidst immensity it towers sublime, —
Winter's eternal palace, built by Time:
All human structures by his touch are borne
Down to the dust; mountains themselves are worn
With his light footsteps; here forever grows,
Amid the region of unmelting snows,
A monument, where every flake that falls
Gives adamantine firmness to the walls.
The sun beholds no mirror, in his race,
That shows a brighter image of his face;
The stars, in their nocturnal vigils, rest
Like signal-fires on its illumined crest;
The gliding moon around the ramparts wheels,
And all its magic lights and shades reveals;
Beneath, the tide with idle fury raves
To undermine it through a thousand caves;

Rent from its roof, though thundering fragments oft
Plunge to the gulf; immovable aloft,
From age to age, in air, o'er sea, on land,
Its turrets heighten, and its piers expand.

Midnight hath told his hour; the moon, yet young,
Hangs in the argent west her bow unstrung;
Larger and fairer, as her lustre fades,
Sparkle the stars amidst the deepening shades:
Jewels, more rich than night's regalia, gem
The distant Ice-Blink's spangled diadem;
Like a new morn from orient darkness, there
Phosphoric splendors kindle in mid-air,
As though from heaven's self-opening portals came
Legions of spirits in an orb of flame, —
Flame, that from every point an arrow sends
Far as the concave firmament extends:
Spun with the tissue of a million lines,
Glistening like gossamer the welkin shines:
The constellations in their pride look pale
Through the quick-trembling brilliance of that veil.
Then, suddenly converged, the meteors rush
O'er the wide south; one deep vermilion blush
O'erspreads Orion glaring on the flood,
And rabid Sirius foams through fire and blood;
Again the circuit of the pole they range,
Motion and figure every moment change,
Through all the colors of the rainbow run,
Or blaze like wrecks of a dissolving sun;
Wide ether burns with glory, conflict, flight,
And the glad ocean dances in the light.

James Montgomery.

PASSING THE ICEBERGS.

A FEARLESS shape of brave device,
   Our vessel drives through mist and rain,
Between the floating fleets of ice, —
   The navies of the northern main.

These arctic ventures, blindly hurled,
   The proofs of Nature's olden force, —
Like fragments of a crystal world
   Long shattered from its skyey course.

These are the buccaneers that fright
   The middle sea with dream of wrecks,
And freeze the south-winds in their flight,
   And chain the Gulf Stream to their decks.

At every dragon prow and helm
   There stands some Viking as of yore;
Grim heroes from the Boreal realm
   Where Odin rules the spectral shore.

And oft beneath the sun or moon
   Their swift and eager falchions glow,
While, like a storm-vexed wind, the rune
   Comes chafing through some beard of snow.

And when the far North flashes up
   With fires of mingled red and gold,
They know that many a blazing cup
   Is brimming to the absent bold.

Up signal there, and let us hail
  Yon looming phantom as we pass!
Note all her fashion, hull, and sail,
  Within the compass of your glass.

See at her mast the steadfast glow
  Of that one star of Odin's throne;
Up with our flag, and let us show
  The constellation on our own.

And speak her well; for she might say,
  If from her heart the words could thaw,
Great news from some far frozen bay,
  Or the remotest Esquimaux:

Might tell of channels yet untold,
  That sweep the pole from sea to sea;
Of lands which God designs to hold
  A mighty people yet to be: —

Of wonders which alone prevail
  Where day and darkness dimly meet;
Of all which spreads the arctic sail;
  Of Franklin and his venturous fleet:

How haply, at some glorious goal
  His anchor holds, his sails are furled;
That Fame has named him on her scroll,
  "Columbus of the Polar World";

Or how his ploughing barques wedge on
  Through splintering fields, with battered shares,

Lit only by that spectral dawn,
    The mask that mocking darkness wears;

Or how, o'er embers black and few,
    The last of shivered masts and spars,
He sits amid his frozen crew
    In council with the Norland stars.

No answer, — but the sullen flow
    Of ocean heaving long and vast;
An argosy of ice and snow,
    The voiceless North swings proudly past.

                    Thomas Buchanan Read.

Sargasso Sea, The.

THE SARGASSO SEA.

"The sailors, according to Herrera, saw the signs of an inundated country (*tierras anegadas*); and it was the general expectation that they should end their lives there, as others had done in the frozen sea, "where Saint Amaro suffers no ship to stir backward or forward." - *Hist del Almirante*, c. 19.

"WHAT vast foundations in the Abyss are there,
    As of a former world? Is it not where
Atlantic kings their barbarous pomp displayed;
Sunk into darkness with the realms they swayed,
When towers and temples, through the closing wave,
A glimmering ray of ancient splendor gave? --
And we shall rest with them. Or are we thrown"

(Each gazed on each, and all exclaimed as one)
"Where things familiar cease and strange begin,
All progress barred to those without, within?
Soon is the doubt resolved.   Arise, behold, —
We stop to stir no more, — nor will the tale be told."
     The pilot smote his breast; the watchman cried
"Land!" and his voice in faltering accents died.
At once the fury of the prow was quelled;
And (whence or why from many an age withheld)
Shrieks, not of men, were mingling in the blast;
And arméd shapes of godlike stature passed!
Slowly along the evening-sky they went,
As on the edge of some vast battlement:
Helmet and shield and spear and gonfalon
Streaming a baleful light that was not of the sun!
     Long from the stern the great Adventurer gazed
With awe, not fear; then high his hands he raised.
"Thou All-Supreme, in goodness as in power,
Who, from his birth to this eventful hour,
Hast led thy servant over land and sea,
Confessing thee in all, and all in thee,
Oh, still —" He spoke, and lo, the charm accurst
Fled whence it came, and the broad barrier burst!
A vain illusion (such as mocks the eyes
Of fearful men, when mountains round them rise
From less than nothing), nothing now beheld
But scattered sedge, — repelling, and repelled!
     And once again that valiant company
Right onward came, ploughing the Unknown Sea.
Already borne beyond the range of thought,
With Light divine and Truth Immortal fraught,

From world to world their steady course they keep,
Swift as the winds along the waters sweep,
Mid the mute nations of the purple deep.
And now the sound of harpy-wings they hear;
Now less and less, as vanishing in fear!
And see, the heavens bow down, the waters rise,
And, rising, shoot in columns to the skies,
That stand, —and still, when they proceed, retire,
As in the Desert burned the sacred fire;
Moving in silent majesty, till night
Descends, and shuts the vision from their sight.

Samuel Rogers.

THE SARGASSO SEA.

IN mid Atlantic are its mazes spread,
  Wide as the basin of our kingly stream;
Barred of all hope which hitherward has led
Do vessels snared within its meshes seem.
Columbus, first to thread this weedy sea,
Thought he had reached here navigation's bound,
But pushing boldly on till all was free,
At length the longed-for, unknown Land he found.
In life's mid-ocean heaves a sea of doubt;
Wise are the souls that past it learn to steer,
Yet tangled there, who toiling struggle out,
Finding once more the ocean's pathway clear,
Look back in triumph on Sargasso passed,
And, though belated, reach the Land at last!

Charlotte Fiske Bates.

GULF-WEED.

A WEARY weed, tossed to and fro,
   Drearily drenched in the ocean brine,
Soaring high and sinking low,
   Lashed along without will of mine;
Sport of the spoom of the surging sea;
   Flung on the foam, afar and anear,
Mark my manifold mystery, —
   Growth and grace in their place appear.

I bear round berries, gray and red,
   Rootless and rover though I be;
My spangled leaves, when nicely spread,
   Arboresce as a trunkless tree;
Corals curious coat me o'er,
   White and hard in apt array;
Mid the wild waves' rude uproar,
   Gracefully grow I, night and day.

Hearts there are on the sounding shore,
   Something whispers soft to me,
Restless and roaming forevermore,
   Like this weary weed of the sea;
Bear they yet on each beating breast
   The eternal type of the wondrous whole:
Growth unfolding amidst unrest,
   Grace informing with silent soul.

Cornelius George Fenner.

Seas of the Tropics.

MORNING AT SEA IN THE TROPICS.

NIGHT waned and wasted, and the fading stars
    Died out like lamps that long survived a feast,
And the moon, pale with watching, sank to rest
Behind the cloud-piled ramparts of the main
Young, blooming Morn, crowned with her bridal wreath,
Bent o'er her mirror clear, the faithful sea,
And gazing on her loveliness therein,
Blushed to the brows, till every imaged charm
Flung roses on the bosom of the wave,
Then, glancing heavenward, both, they blushed again,
As sprang the Sun to claim his radiant bride;
And sea and sky seemed but one rose of morn.
Which thenceforth grew in glory, and the world
Shot back her lesser light upon the day,
While night sped on to seek the sombre shades
That sleep in silent caves beyond the sea.
The day grew calmer, hotter, and our barque
Lay like a sleeping swan upon a lake,
And such soft airs as blew from off the land
Brought with them fragrant odors, and we felt
That orange groves lay blooming 'neath the sun
Which blazed so fiercely overhead at sea.
We heard (with Fancy's ear) a distant bell;
And through the haze that simmered on the main
Pictured a purple shore, — a convent tower

And snowy cots, that from the dark hillside
Peeped forth 'tween plantain-patches at the sky,
Or smiled through groves of cocoas on the sea.
Meanwhile our ship slid on, with breathing sails
Fraught with the melody of murmured song
Such as the zephyr chanted to the morn,
And showers of diamonds flashed before the prow,
While sternwards whirled unstrung pale beads of
        foam, —
Pearls from the loosened chaplet of the sea.
-Mid these the flame-bright Nautilus, that seemed
Itself a floweret cast upon the stream,
Spread out its crimson sail and drifted on.
Beyond arose a cloud (as 't were) of birds,
That leaped from out the wave to meet the sun,
Flew a short circuit, till their wings grew dry,
And seaward fell in showers of silver rain.
Mid these careered the dolphin-squadrons swift,
With mail of changeful hue, and Iris tints;
And floating slowly on, a sea-flower passed,
A living creature (none the less a flower)
That lives its life in love, and dies for joy,
Unmissed mid myriads in the sapphire sea.

George Gordon McCrae.

THE TORRID ZONE.

NOW come, bold Fancy, spread a daring flight,
    And view the wonders of the Torrid Zone:
Climes unrelenting! with whose rage compared,
You blaze is feeble, and you skies are cool.

See, how at once the bright effulgent sun,
Rising, direct, swift chases from the sky
The short-lived twilight; and with ardent blaze
Looks gayly fierce o'er all the dazzling air:
He mounts his throne; but kind before him sends,
Issuing from out the portals of the morn,
The gentle breeze, to mitigate his fire,
And breathe refreshment on a fainting world.
Great are the scenes, with dreadful beauty crowned
And barbarous wealth, that see, each circling year,
Returning suns and double seasons pass:
Rocks rich in gems, and mountains big with mines,
That on the high equator ridgy rise,
Whence many a bursting stream auriferous plays:
Majestic woods, of every vigorous green,
Stage above stage, high waving o'er the hills;
Or to the far horizon wide diffused,
A boundless deep immensity of shade.
Here lofty trees, to ancient song unknown,
The noble sons of potent heat and floods
Prone-rushing from the clouds, rear high to heaven
Their thorny stems, and broad around them throw
Meridian gloom. Here, in eternal prime,
Unnumbered fruits of keen delicious taste
And vital spirit, drink amid the cliffs,
And burning sands that bank the shrubby vales,
Redoubled day, yet in their rugged coats
A friendly juice to cool its rage contain.

  Bear me, Pomona! to thy citron groves;
To where the lemon and the piercing lime,
With the deep orange, glowing through the green,

Their lighter glories blend. Lay me reclined
Beneath the spreading tamarind that shakes,
Fanned by the breeze, its fever-cooling fruit.
Deep in the night the massy locust sheds,
Quench my hot limbs; or lead me through the maze,
Embowering endless, of the Indian fig;
Or thrown at gayer ease, on some fair brow,
Let me behold, by breezy murmurs cooled,
Broad o'er my head the verdant cedar wave,
And high palmettos lift their graceful shade.
Or stretched amid these orchards of the sun,
Give me to drain the cocoa's milky bowl,
And from the palm to draw its freshening wine!
More bounteous far than all the frantic juice
Which Bacchus pours. Nor, on its slender twigs
Low-bending, be the full pomegranate scorned;
Nor, creeping through the woods, the gelid race
Of berries. Oft in humble station dwells
Unboasted worth, above fastidious pomp.
Witness, thou best Anana, thou the pride
Of vegetable life, beyond whate'er
The poets imaged in the Golden Age:
Quick let me strip thee of thy tufty coat,
Spread thy ambrosial stores, and feast with Jove!
　　From these the prospect varies. Plains immense
Lie stretched below, interminable meads,
And vast savannas, where the wandering eye,
Unfixed, is in a verdant ocean lost.
Another Flora there, of bolder hues
And richer sweets, beyond our garden's pride,
Plays o'er the fields, and showers with sudden hand

Exuberant spring; for oft these valleys shift
Their green embroidered robe to fiery brown,
And swift to green again, as scorching suns
Or streaming dews and torrent rains prevail.
Along these lonely regions, where, retired
From little scenes of art, great Nature dwells
In awful solitude, and naught is seen
But the wild herds that own no master's stall,
Prodigious rivers roll their fattening seas:
On whose luxuriant herbage, half concealed,
Like a fallen cedar, far diffused his train,
Cased in green scales, the crocodile extends.
The flood disparts: behold! in plaited mail
Behemoth rears his head. Glanced from his side,
The darted steel in idle shivers flies:
He fearless walks the plain, or seeks the hills;
Where, as he crops his varied fare, the herds,
In widening circle round, forget their food,
And at the harmless stranger wondering gaze.

    Peaceful, beneath primeval trees, that cast
Their ample shade o'er Niger's yellow stream,
And where the Ganges rolls his sacred wave;
Or mid the central depth of blackening woods,
High raised in solemn theatre around,
Leans the huge elephant: wisest of brutes!
O truly wise, with gentle might endowed,
Though powerful, not destructive! here he sees
Revolving ages sweep the changeful earth,
And empires rise and fall; regardless he
Of what the never-resting race of men
Project: thrice happy! could he 'scape their guile

Who mine, from cruel avarice, his steps;
Or with his towery grandeur swell their state,
The pride of kings! or else his strength pervert,
And bid him rage amid the mortal fray,
Astonished at the madness of mankind.

Wide o'er the winding umbrage of the floods,
Like vivid blossoms glowing from afar,
Thick swarm the brighter birds. For Nature's hand,
That with a sportive vanity has decked
The plumy nations, there her gayest hues
Profusely pours. But, if she bids them shine,
Arrayed in all the beauteous beams of day,
Yet frugal still, she humbles them in song.

James Thomson.

TYPHON AND ECNEPHIA.

IN the dread ocean, undulating wide,
Beneath the radiant line that girts the globe,
The circling Typhon, whirled from point to point,
Exhausting all the rage of all the sky,
And dire Ecnephia reign. Amid the heavens,
Falsely serene, deep in a cloudy speck
Compressed, the mighty tempest brooding dwells.
Of no regard, save to the skilful eye,
Fiery and foul, the small prognostic hangs
Aloft, or on the promontory's brow
Musters its force. A faint deceitful calm,
A fluttering gale, the demon sends before,
To tempt the spreading sail. Then down at once,
Precipitant, descends a mingled mass

Of roaring winds, and flame, and rushing floods.
In wild amazement fixed the sailor stands.
Art is too slow. By rapid fate oppressed,
His broad-winged vessel drinks the whelming tide,
Hid in the bosom of the black abyss.

James Thomson.

TROPICAL WEATHER.

NOW we 're afloat upon the tropic sea ;
Here Summer holdeth a perpetual reign.
How flash the waters in their bounding glee !
The sky's soft purple is without a stain.
Full in our wake the smooth, warm trade-winds, blowing,
To their unvarying goal still faithful run ;
And, as we steer, with sails before them flowing,
Nearer the zenith daily climbs the sun.
The startled flying-fish around us skim,
Glossed, like the humming-bird, with rainbow dyes,
And, as they dip into the water's brim,
Swift in pursuit the preying dolphin hies.
All, all is fair ; and, gazing round, we feel
Over the yielding sense the torrid languor steal.

Epes Sargent

Ocean, and sky, and earth — a blistering calm
Spread over all! How weary wears the day!
Oh, lift the wave, and bend the distant palm,
Breeze! wheresoe'er thy lagging pinions stay!
Triumphant burst upon the level deep,
Rock the fixed hull and stretch the clinging sail!
Arouse the opal clouds that o'er us sleep!
Sound thy shrill whistle! we will bid thee hail!
Though wrapped in all the storm-clouds of the North,
Yet, from thy home of ice, come forth, O breeze, come
       forth!

Epes Sargent.

TROPICAL NIGHT.

BUT oh, the night, — the cool, luxurious night,
   Which closes round us when the day grows dim,
And the sun sinks from his meridian height
Behind the ocean's occidental rim!
Clouds in thin streaks of purple, green, and red,
Lattice his dying glory, and absorb —
Hung o'er his couch — the rallying lustre shed,
Like love's last tender glances, from his orb.
And now the moon, her lids unclosing, deigns
To smile serenely on the charmèd sea,
That shines as if inlaid with lightning-chains,
From which it faintly struggled to be free.
Swan-like, with motion unperceived, we glide,
Touched by the downy breeze, and favored by the tide.

Epes Sargent.

THE LOTOS-EATERS.

"COURAGE!" he said, and pointed toward the land,
   "This mounting wave will roll us shoreward soon."
In the afternoon they came unto a land,
   In which it seemed always afternoon.
All round the coast the languid air did swoon,
   Breathing like one that hath a weary dream.
Full-faced above the valley stood the moon;
   And like a downward smoke, the slender stream
Along the cliff to fall, and pause, and fall did seem.

A land of streams! some, like a downward smoke,
   Slow-dropping veils of thinnest lawn, did go;
And some through wavering lights and shadows broke,
   Rolling a slumbrous sheet of foam below.
They saw the gleaming river seaward flow
   From the inner land: far off, three mountain-tops,
Three silent pinnacles of aged snow,
   Stood sunset-flushed: and, dewed with showery drops,
Up-clomb the shadowy pine above the woven copse.

The charmed sunset lingered low adown
   In the red West: through mountain clefts the dale
Was seen far inland, and the yellow down
   Bordered with palm, and many a winding vale
And meadow, set with slender galingale;
   A land where all things always seemed the same!
And round about the keel with faces pale,

Dark faces pale against that rosy flame,
The mild-eyed melancholy Lotos-eaters came.

Branches they bore of that enchanted stem,
Laden with flower and fruit, whereof they gave
To each, but whoso did receive of them,
And taste, to him the gushing of the wave
Far far away did seem to mourn and rave,
On alien shores; and if his fellow spake,
His voice was thin, as voices from the grave;
And deep-asleep he seemed yet all awake,
And music in his ears his beating heart did make.
They sat them down upon the yellow sand
Between the sun and moon upon the shore;
And sweet it was to dream of Fatherland,
Of child, and wife, and slave: but evermore
Most weary seemed the sea, weary the oar,
Weary the wandering fields of barren foam.
Then some one said, "We will return no more";
And all at once they sang, "Our island home
Is far beyond the wave; we will no longer roam."

*　　　　*　　　　*

The Lotos blooms below the barren peak:
The Lotos blows by every winding creek:
All day the wind breathes low with mellower tone:
Through every hollow cave and alley lone
Round and round the spicy downs the yellow Lotos-
　　　dust is blown.
We have had enough of action, and of motion we,

Rolled to starboard, rolled to larboard, when the surge
    was seething free,
Where the wallowing monster spouted his foam-foun-
    tains in the sea.

                               Alfred Tennyson.

Atlantic Ocean.

THE SAILING OF ULYSSES.

                           WHEN I

From Circe had departed, who concealed me
    More than a year there near unto Gaeta,
    Or ever yet Æneas named it so,
Nor fondness for my son, nor reverence
    For my old father, nor the due affection
    Which joyous should have made Penelope,
Could overcome within me the desire
    I had to be experienced of the world,
    And of the vice and virtue of mankind;
But I put forth on the high open sea
    With one sole ship, and that small company
    By which I never had deserted been.
Both of the shores I saw as far as Spain,
    Far as Morocco, and the isle of Sardes,
    And the others which that sea bathes round about.
I and my company were old and slow
    When at that narrow passage we arrived
    Where Hercules his landmarks set as signals,

That man no farther onward should adventure.
    On the right hand behind me left I Seville,
    And on the other already had left Ceuta.
"O brothers, who amid a hundred thousand
    Perils," I said, "have come unto the West,
    To this so inconsiderable vigil
Which is remaining of your senses still,
    Be ye unwilling to deny the knowledge,
    Following the sun, of the unpeopled world.
Consider ye the seed from which ye sprang;
    Ye were not made to live like unto brutes,
    But for pursuit of virtue and of knowledge."
So eager did I render my companions,
    With this brief exhortation, for the voyage,
    That then I hardly could have held them back.
And having turned our stern unto the morning,
    We of the oars made wings for our mad flight,
    Evermore gaining on the larboard side.
Already all the stars of the other pole
    The night beheld, and ours so very low
    It did not rise above the ocean floor.
Five times rekindled and as many quenched
    Had been the splendor underneath the moon,
    Since we had entered into the deep pass,
When there appeared to us a mountain, dim
    From distance, and it seemed to me so high
    As I had never any one beheld.
Joyful were we, and soon it turned to weeping;
    For out of the new land a whirlwind rose,
    And smote upon the forepart of the ship.
Three times it made her whirl with all the waters,

At the fourth time it made the stern uplift,

And the prow downward go, as pleased Another,
Until the sea above us closed again.

Dante Alighieri. Tr. H. W. Longfellow.

ULYSSES.

IT little profits that an idle king,
By this still hearth, among these barren crags,
Matched with an aged wife, I mete and dole
Unequal laws unto a savage race,
That hoard, and sleep, and feed, and know not me.
I cannot rest from travel: I will drink
Life to the lees: all times I have enjoyed
Greatly, have suffered greatly, both with those
That loved me, and alone; on shore, and when
Through scudding drifts the rainy Hyades
Vext the dim sea: I am become a name;
For always roaming with a hungry heart
Much have I seen and known; cities of men
And manners, climates, councils, governments,
Myself not least, but honored of them all,
And drunk delight of battle with my peers,
Far on the ringing plains of windy Troy.
I am a part of all that I have met;
Yet all experience is an arch wherethrough
Gleams that untravelled world, whose margin fades
Forever and forever when I move.
How dull it is to pause, to make an end,
To rust unburnished, not to shine in use!

As though to breathe were life. Life piled on life
Were all too little, and of one to me
Little remains : but every hour is saved
From that eternal silence, something more,
A bringer of new things; and vile it were
For some three suns to store and hoard myself,
And this gray spirit yearning in desire
To follow knowledge, like a sinking star,
Beyond the utmost bound of human thought.

    This is my son, mine own Telemachus,
To whom I leave the sceptre and the isle —
Well loved of me, discerning to fulfil
This labor, by slow prudence to make mild
A rugged people, and through soft degrees
Subdue them to the useful and the good.
Most blameless is he, centred in the sphere
Of common duties, decent not to fail
In offices of tenderness, and pay
Meet adoration to my household gods
When I am gone. He works his work, I mine.

    There lies the port: the vessel puffs her sail:
There gloom the dark broad seas. My mariners,
Souls that have toiled, and wrought, and thought with
     me —
That ever with a frolic welcome took
The thunder and the sunshine, and opposed
Free hearts, free foreheads — you and I are old;
Old age hath yet his honor and his toil;
Death closes all : but something ere the end,
Some work of noble note, may yet be done,
Not unbecoming men that strove with gods.

The lights begin to twinkle from the rocks:
The long day wanes: the slow moon climbs: the deep
Moans round with many voices. Come, my friends,
'T is not too late to seek a newer world.
Push off, and sitting well in order smite
The sounding furrows; for my purpose holds
To sail beyond the sunset, and the baths
Of all the western stars, until I die.
It may be that the gulfs will wash us down:
It may be we shall touch the Happy Isles,
And see the great Achilles, whom we knew.
Though much is taken, much abides; and though
We are not now that strength which in old days
Moved earth and heaven, that which we are, we are;
One equal temper of heroic hearts,
Made weak by time and fate, but strong in will
To strive, to seek, to find, and not to yield.

Alfred Tennyson

ON A ROCK IN THE ATLANTIC.

HERE in this solemn spot, from hour to hour,
From age to age, earth and the mighty sea
Fight for dominion. Here — where none can see,
None hear, none aid, —when autumn tempests lower,
And the wild winds strike loud their stormy drums,
Forth from his caves the blown Atlantic comes,
Scattering his foaming fury, night by night,
'Gainst the scarred basalt's all enduring might.
Stern foes! who fight for lords ye never saw
Not vain your noise, if from the unending strife

A peaceful lesson clamorous man would draw,
And thereby learn to sheathe his useless knife;
Or must ye both still set life against life,
Obeying thus some wise but unknown law?

Bryan Waller Procter.

SEAWEED.

WHEN descends on the Atlantic
          The gigantic
Storm-wind of the equinox,
Landward in his wrath he scourges
          The toiling surges,
Laden with seaweed from the rocks:

From Bermuda's reefs; from edges
          Of sunken ledges,
In some far-off, bright Azore;
From Bahama, and the dashing,
          Silver-flashing
Surges of San Salvador;

From the tumbling surf, that buries
          The Orkneyan skerries,
Answering the hoarse Hebrides;
And from wrecks of ships, and drifting
          Spars, uplifting
On the desolate, rainy seas; —

Ever drifting, drifting, drifting
          On the shifting

Currents of the restless main;
Till in sheltered coves, and reaches
    Of sandy beaches,
All have found repose again.

So when storms of wild emotion
    Strike the ocean
Of the poet's soul, erelong
From each cave and rocky fastness,
    In its vastness,
Floats some fragment of a song;

From the far-off isles enchanted,
    Heaven has planted
With the golden fruit of Truth;
From the flashing surf, whose vision
    Gleams Elysian
In the tropic clime of Youth;

From the strong Will, and the endeavor
    That forever
Wrestles with the tides of Fate;
From the wreck of Hopes far-scattered,
    Tempest-shattered,
Floating waste and desolate; —

Ever drifting, drifting, drifting
    On the shifting
Currents of the restless heart;
Till at length in books recorded,
    They, like hoarded
Household words, no more depart.

Henry Wadsworth Longfellow.

THE SHIP OF THE DEAD.

AND now along the horizon's edge
   Mountains of cloud uprose,
Black as with forests underneath,
Above, their sharp and jagged teeth
   Were white as drifted snows.

Unseen behind them sank the sun,
   But flushed each snowy peak
A little while with rosy light
That faded slowly from the sight
   As blushes from the cheek.

Black grew the sky, — all black, all black;
   The clouds were everywhere;
There was a feeling of suspense
In nature, a mysterious sense
   Of terror in the air.

And all on board the Valdemar
   Was still as still could be;
Save when the dismal ship-bell tolled,
As ever and anon she rolled,
   And lurched into the sea.

The captain up and down the deck
   Went striding to and fro;
Now watched the compass at the wheel,
Now lifted up his hand to feel
   Which way the wind might blow.

And now he looked up at the sails,
　And now upon the deep;
In every fibre of his frame
He felt the storm before it came,
　He had no thought of sleep.

Eight bells! and suddenly abaft,
　With a great rush of rain,
Making the ocean white with spume,
In darkness like the day of doom,
　On came the hurricane.

The lightning flashed from cloud to cloud,
　And rent the sky in two;
A jagged flame, a single jet
Of white fire, like a bayonet,
　That pierced the eyeballs through.

Then all around is dark again,
　And blacker than before;
But in that single flash of light
He had beheld a fearful sight,
　And thought of the oath he swore.

For right ahead lay the Ship of the Dead,
　The ghostly Carmilhan!
Her masts were stripped, her yards were bare,
And on her bowsprit, poised in air,
　Sat the Klaboterman.

Her crew of ghosts was all on deck
　Or clambering up the shrouds;
The boatswain's whistle, the captain's hail

Were like the piping of the gale,
  And thunder in the clouds.

And close behind the Carmilhan
  There rose up from the sea,
As from a foundered ship of stone,
Three bare and splintered masts alone:
  They were the Chimneys Three.

And onward dashed the Valdemar
  And leaped into the dark;
A denser mist, a colder blast,
A little shudder, and she had passed
  Right through the Phantom Bark.

She cleft in twain the shadowy hulk,
  But cleft it unaware;
As when, careering to her nest,
The sea-gull severs with her breast
  The unresisting air.

Again the lightning flashed; again
  They saw the Carmilhan,
Whole as before in hull and spar;
But now on board of the Valdemar
  Stood the Klaboterman.

And they all knew their doom was sealed;
  They knew that death was near;
Some prayed who never prayed before,
And some they wept, and some they swore,
  And some were mute with fear.

Then suddenly there came a shock,
  And louder than wind or sea
A cry burst from the crew on deck,
As she dashed and crashed, a hopeless wreck,
  Upon the Chimneys Three.

The storm and night were passed, the light
  To streak the east began;
The cabin boy, picked up at sea,
Survived the wreck, and only he,
  To tell of the Carmilhan.

Henry Wadsworth Longfellow.

Indian Ocean.

INDIAN OCEAN.

BEHIND them now the Cape of Prasa bends,
  Another ocean to their view extends,
Where black-topped islands, to their longing eyes,
Laved by the gentle waves, in prospect rise.
But Gama captain of the venturous band,
Of bold emprize, and born for high command,
Whose martial fire, with prudence close allied,
Insured the smiles of Fortune on his side,
Bears off those shores which waste and wild appeared,
And eastward still for happier climates steered.
When gathering round, and blackening o'er the tide,
A fleet of small canoes the pilot spied:
Hoisting their sails of palm-tree leaves, inwove

With curious art, a swarming crowd they move:
Long were their boats, and sharp to bound along
Through the dashed waters, broad their oars and strong:
The bending rowers on their features bore
The swarthy marks of Phaeton's fall of yore:
When flaming lightnings scorched the banks of Po,
And nations blackened in the dread o'erthrow.
Their garb, discovered as approaching nigh,
Was cotton striped with many a gaudy dye:
'T was one whole piece beneath one arm confined,
The rest hung loose and fluttered on the wind;
All, but one breast, above the loins was bare,
And swelling turbans bound their jetty hair:
Their arms were bearded darts and falchions broad,
And warlike music sounded as they rowed.
With joy the sailors saw the boats draw near,
With joy beheld the human face appear:
What nations these, their wondering thoughts explore,
What rites they follow, and what God adore!
And now with hands and kerchiefs waved in air
The barbarous race their friendly mind declare.
Glad were the crew, and weened that happy day
Should end their dangers and their toils repay.
The lofty masts the nimble youths ascend,
The ropes they haul, and o'er the yard-arms bend;
And now their bowsprits pointing to the shore,
(A safe, moored bay), with slackened sails they bore:
With cheerful shouts they furl the gathered sail
That less and less flaps quivering on the gale;
The prows, their speed stopped, o'er the surges nod,
The falling anchors dash the foaming flood;

When, sudden as they stopped, the swarthy race,
With smiles of friendly welcome on each face,
The ship's high sides swift by the cordage climb:
Illustrious Gama, with an air sublime,
Softened by mild humanity, receives,
And to their chief the hand of friendship gives,
Bids spread the board, and, instant as he said,
Along the deck the festive board is spread:
The sparkling wine in crystal goblets glows,
And round and round with cheerful welcome flows.

Luis de Camoens. Tr. W. J. Mickle.

———•◦•———

Pacific Ocean.

LINES

WRITTEN IN A BLANK LEAF OF LA PÉROUSE'S VOYAGES.

L OVED Voyager! his pages had a zest
More sweet than fiction to my wondering breast,
When, rapt in fancy, many a boyish day
I tracked his wanderings o'er the watery way,
Roamed round the Aleutian isles in waking dreams,
Or plucked the fleur-de-lys by Jesso's streams,
Or gladly leaped on that far Tartar strand
Where Europe's anchor ne'er had bit the sand,
Where scarce a roving wild tribe crossed the plain,
Or human voice broke nature's silent reign;
But vast and grassy deserts feed the bear,
And sweeping deer-herds dread no hunter's snare.

Such young delight his real records brought,
His truth so touched romantic springs of thought,
That all my after-life his fate and fame
Entwined romance with La Pérouse's name.
Fair were his ships, expert his gallant crews,
And glorious the enterprise of La Pérouse, —
Humanely glorious! Men will weep for him,
When many a guilty martial fame is dim:
He ploughed the deep to bind no captive's chain,
Pursued no rapine, strewed no wreck with slain;
And, save that in the deep themselves lie low,
His heroes plucked no wreath from human woe.
'T was his the earth's remotest bound to scan,
Conciliating with gifts barbaric man, —
Enrich the world's contemporaneous mind,
And amplify the picture of mankind.
Far on the vast Pacific, midst those isles,
O'er which the earliest morn of Asia smiles,
He sounded and gave charts to many a shore
And gulf of ocean new to nautic lore;
Yet he that led discovery o'er the wave
Still fills himself an undiscovered grave.
He came not back, — Conjecture's cheek grew pale,
Year after year, — in no propitious gale
His lilied banner held its homeward way,
And Science saddened at her martyr's stay.

An age elapsed, — no wreck told where or when
The chief went down with all his gallant men,
Or whether by the storm and wild sea flood
He perished, or by wilder men of blood:

The shuddering Fancy only guessed his doom,
And Doubt to Sorrow gave but deeper gloom.
An age elapsed, — when men were dead or gray.
Whose hearts had mourned him in their youthful day,
Fame traced, on Mannicolo's shore, at last,
The boiling surge had mounted o'er his mast,
The islesmen told of some surviving men,
But Christian eyes beheld them ne'er again.
Sad bourn of all his toils — with all his band —
To sleep, wrecked, shroudless, on a savage strand!
Yet what is all that fires a hero's scorn
Of death? — the hope to live in hearts unborn:
Life to the brave is not its fleeting breath,
But worth — foretasting fame, that follows death.
That worth had La Pérouse, that meed he won;
He sleeps, his life's long stormy watch is done.
In the great deep, whose boundaries and space
He measured, Fate ordained his resting-place;
But bade his fame, like the ocean rolling o'er
His relics, visit every earthly shore.
Fair Science, on that ocean's azure robe,
Still writes his name in picturing the globe,
And paints (what fairer wreath could glory twine?)
His watery course, — a world-encircling line.

Thomas Campbell.

SOUTHERN SEAS.

YES! let us mount this gallant ship:
  Spread canvas to the wind, —
Up! we will seek the glowing South, —
Leave care and cold behind.

Let the shark pursue through the waters blue
Our flying vessel's track;
Let strong winds blow, and rocks below
Threaten, — we turn not back.

Trusting in Him who holds the sea
In his Almighty hand,
We pass the awful waters wide,
Tread many a far-off strand.

Right onward as our course we hold,
From day to day, the sky
Above our head its arch shall spread
More glowing, bright, and high;

And from night to night — oh, what delight!
In its azure depths to mark
Stars all unknown come glittering out
Over the ocean dark.

The moon uprising like a sun,
So stately, large, and sheen,
And the very stars, like clustered moons,
In the crystal ether keen.

Whilst all about the ship, below,
Strange, fiery billows play, —
The ceaseless keel through liquid fire
Cuts wondrously its way.

But oh, the South! the balmy South!
How warm the breezes float!
How warm the amber waters stream
From off our basking boat!

Come down, come down from the tall ship's side, —
What a marvellous sight is here!
Look! purple rocks and crimson trees,
Down in the deep so clear.

See! where those shoals of dolphins go,
A glad and glorious band,
Sporting amongst the roseate woods
Of a coral fairy-land.

See! on the violet sands beneath
How the gorgeous shells do glide!
O sea! old sea, who yet knows half
Of thy wonders and thy pride!

Look how the sea-plants trembling float,
As it were like a mermaid's locks,
Waving in thread of ruby red
Over those nether rocks,

Heaving and sinking, soft and fair,
Here hyacinth, there green, –
With many a stem of golden growth,
And starry flowers between.

But away! away to upper day!
For monstrous shapes are here, —
Monsters of dark and wallowing bulk,
And horny eyeballs drear:

The tuskéd mouth, and the spiny fin,
Speckled and warted back;
The glittering swift, and the flabby slow,
Ramp through this deep sea track.

Away! away! to upper day,
To glance o'er the breezy brine,
And see the nautilus gladly sail,
The flying-fish leap and shine.

But what is that? "'T is land! 'T is land!
'T is land!" the sailors cry.
Nay! 't is a long and a narrow cloud
Betwixt the sea and sky.

"'T is land! 't is land!" they cry once more;
And now comes breathing on
An odor of the living earth,
Such as the sea hath none.

But now I mark the rising shores!
The purple hills! the trees!
Ah! what a glorious land is here,
What happy scenes are these!

See! how the tall palms lift their locks
From mountain clefts, — what vales,
Basking beneath the noontide sun,
That high and hotly sails.

Yet all about the breezy shore,
Unheedful of the glow,
Look how the children of the South
Are passing to and fro!

What noble forms! what fairy place!
Cast anchor in this cove,
Push out the boat, for in this land
A little we must rove!

We 'll wander on through wood and field,
We 'll sit beneath the vine ;
We 'll drink the limpid cocoa-milk,
And pluck the native pine.

The bread-fruit and cassada-root,
And many a glowing berry,
Shall be our feast ; for here, at least,
Why should we not be merry !

For 't is a southern paradise,
All gladsome, — plain and shore, —
A land so far that here we are,
But shall be here no more.

We 've seen the splendid southern clime.
Its seas and isles and men ;
So now ! back to a dearer land, —
To England back again !

William Howitt.

SOUTH SEA ISLANDS.

OH, many are the beauteous isles
Unknown to human eye,
That, sleeping mid the Ocean smiles.
In happy silence lie.
The ship may pass them in the night.
Nor the sailors know what a lovely sight
Is resting on the main. -
Some wandering ship who hath lost her way,

And never, or by night or day,
Shall pass these isles again.
There, groves that bloom in endless spring
Are rustling to the radiant wing
Of birds, in various plumage, bright
As rainbow-hues or dawning light.
Soft-falling showers of blossoms fair
Float ever on the fragrant air,
Like showers of vernal snow,
And from the fruit-tree, spreading tall,
The richly ripened clusters fall
Oft as sea-breezes blow.
The sun and clouds alone possess
The joy of all that loveliness;
And sweetly to each other smile
The live-long day, — sun, cloud, and isle.
How silent lies each sheltered bay!
No other visitors have they
To their shores of silvery sand,
Than the waves that, murmuring in their glee,
All hurrying in a joyful band
Come dancing from the sea.

    How did I love to sigh and weep
For those that sailed upon the deep,
When, yet a wondering child,
I sat alone at dead of night,
Hanging all breathless with delight
O'er their adventures wild!
Trembling I heard of dizzy shrouds,
Where up among the raving clouds

The sailor-boy must go ;
Thunder and lightning o'er his head !
And should he fall — oh thought of dread !
Waves mountain-high below.
How leapt my heart with wildering fears,
Gazing on savage islanders
Ranged fierce in long canoe,
Their poisoned spears, their war-attire,
And plumes twined bright, like wreaths of fire,
Round brows of dusky hue !
What tears would fill my wakeful eyes
When some delicious paradise
(As if a cloud had rolled
On a sudden from the bursting sun),
Freshening the Ocean where it shone,
Flung wide its groves of gold !
No more the pining mariner
In wild delirium raves,
For like an angel, kind and fair,
That smiles and smiling saves,
The glory charms away distress,
Serene in silent loveliness
Amid the dash of waves.

John Wilson.

A DESERT ISLAND.

THE mountain wooded to the peak, the lawns
And winding glades high up like ways to heaven,
The slender coco's drooping crown of plumes,
The lightning flash of insect and of bird,

The lustre of the long convolvuluses,
That coiled around the stately stems, and ran
Even to the limit of the land, the glows
And glories of the broad belt of the world, —
All these he saw; but what he fain had seen
He could not see, the kindly human face,
Nor ever hear a kindly voice, but heard
The myriad shriek of wheeling ocean-fowl,
The league-long roller thundering on the reef,
The moving whisper of huge trees that branched
And blossomed in the zenith, or the sweep
Of some precipitous rivulet to the wave,
As down the shores he ranged, or all day long
Sat often in the seaward-gazing gorge,
A shipwrecked sailor, waiting for a sail:
No sail from day to day, but every day
The sunrise broken into scarlet shafts
Among the palms and ferns and precipices;
The blaze upon the waters to the east;
The blaze upon his island overhead;
The blaze upon the waters to the west;
Then the great stars that globed themselves in heaven,
The hollower-bellowing ocean, and again
The scarlet shafts of sunrise, — but no sail.

Alfred Tennyson.

The Ocean.

THE VOYAGE OF VASCO DE GAMA.

FROM Leo now, the lordly star of day,
Intensely blazing, shot his fiercest ray;
When, slowly gliding from our wishful eyes,
The Lusian mountains mingled with the skies;
Tago's loved stream, and Cintra's mountains cold
Dim fading now, we now no more behold;
And, still with yearning hearts our eyes explore,
Till one dim speck of land appears no more.
Our native soil now far behind, we ply
The lonely, dreary waste of seas, and boundless sky.
Through the wild deep our venturous navy bore,
Where but our Henry ploughed the wave before;
The verdant islands, first by him descried,
We passed; and, now in prospect opening wide,
Far to the left, increasing on the view,
Rose Mauritania's hills of paly blue:
Far to the right the restless ocean roared,
Whose bounding surges never keel explored:
If bounding shore (as reason deems) divide
The vast Atlantic from the Indian tide.

Named from her woods, with fragrant bowers adorned,
From fair Madeira's purple coast we turned:
Cyprus and Paphos' vales the smiling loves
Might leave with joy for fair Madeira's groves;

A shore so flowery, and so sweet an air,
Venus might build her dearest temple there.
Onward we pass Massilia's barren strand,
A waste of withered grass and burning sand;
Where his thin herds the meagre native leads,
Where not a rivulet laves the doleful meads;
Nor herds nor fruitage deck the woodland maze;
O'er the wild waste the stupid ostrich strays,
In devious search to pick her scanty meal,
Whose fierce digestion gnaws the tempered steel.
From the green verge, where Tigitania ends,
To Ethiopia's line the dreary wild extends.

Now, past the limit which his course divides,
When to the north the sun's bright chariot rides,
We leave the winding bays and swarthy shores,
Where Senegal's black wave impetuous roars;
A flood, whose course a thousand tribes surveys,
The tribes who blackened in the fiery blaze
When Phaeton, devious from the solar height,
Gave Afric's sons the sable hue of night.
And now, from far the Libyan cape is seen,
Now by my mandate named the Cape of Green;
Where, midst the billows of the ocean, smiles
A flowery sister-train, the Happy Isles,
Our onward prows the murmuring surges lave;
And now, our vessels plough the gentle wave,
Where the blue islands, named of Hesper old,
Their fruitful bosoms to the deep unfold.
Here, changeful Nature shows her various face,
And frolics o'er the slopes with wildest grace:

Here, our bold fleet their ponderous anchors threw,
The sickly cherish, and our stores renew.
From him, the warlike guardian power of Spain,
Whose spear's dread lightning o'er the embattled
    plain
Has oft o'erwhelmed the Moors in dire dismay,
And fixed the fortune of the doubtful day;
From him we name our station of repair,
And Jago's name that isle shall ever bear.
The northern winds now curled the blackening main,
Our sails unfurled, we plough the tide again:
Round Afric's coast our winding course we steer,
Where, bending to the east, the shores appear.
Here, Jalofo its wide extent displays,
And vast Mandinga shows its numerous bays;
Whose mountains' sides, though parched and barren,
    hold,
In copious store, the seeds of beamy gold.
The Gambia here his serpent-journey takes,
And through the lawns a thousand windings makes;
A thousand swarthy tribes his current laves
Ere mix his waters with the Atlantic waves.
The Gorgades we passed, that hated shore,
Famed for its terrors by the bards of yore;
Where but one eye by Phorcus' daughters shared,
The 'lorn beholders into marble stared;
Three dreadful sisters' down whose temples rolled
Their hair of snakes in many a hissing fold,
And, scattering horror o'er the dreary strand,
With swarms of vipers sowed the burning sand.
Still to the south our pointed keels we guide,

And through the austral gulf still onward ride :
Her palmy forests mingling with the skies,
Leona's rugged steep behind us flies ;
The Cape of Palms that jutting land we name,
Already conscious of our nation's fame.
Where the vexed waves against our bulwarks roar,
And Lusian towers o'erlook the bending shore :
Our sails wide swelling to the constant blast,
Now by the isle from Thomas named we passed ;
And Congo's spacious realm before us rose,
Where copious Layra's limpid billow flows ;
A flood by ancient hero never seen,
Where many a temple o'er the banks of green,
Reared by the Lusian heroes, through the night
Of pagan darkness, pours the mental light.

O'er the wild waves, as southward thus we stray,
Our port unknown, unknown the watery way,
Each night we see, impressed with solemn awe,
Our guiding stars, and native skies withdraw,
In the wide void we lose their cheering beams,
Lower and lower still the pole-star gleams.
Till past the limit, where the car of day
Rolled o'er our heads, and poured the downward ray :
We now disprove the faith of ancient lore ;
Boötes' shining car appears no more.
For here we saw Calisto's star retire
Beneath the waves, unawed by Juno's ire.
Here, while the sun his polar journeys takes,
His visit doubled, double season makes ;
Stern winter twice deforms the changeful year,

And twice the spring's gay flowers their honors rear.
Now, pressing onward, past the burning zone,
Beneath another heaven and stars unknown,
Unknown to heroes and to sages old,
With southward prows our pathless course we hold :
Here, gloomy night assumes a darker reign,
And fewer stars emblaze the heavenly plain ;
Fewer than those that gild the northern pole,
And o'er our seas their glittering chariots roll ;
While nightly thus, the lonely seas we brave,
Another pole-star rises o'er the wave :
Full to the south a shining cross appears,
Our heaving breasts the blissful omen cheers :
Seven radiant stars compose the hallowed sign
That rose still higher o'er the wavy brine.
Beneath this southern axle of the world
Never, with daring search, was flag unfurled ;
Nor pilot knows if bounding shores are placed,
Or, if one dreary sea o'erflow the lonely waste.

While thus our keels still onward boldly strayed,
Now tossed by tempests, now by calms delayed,
To tell the terrors of the deep untried,
What toils we suffered, and what storms defied ;
What rattling deluges the black clouds poured,
What dreary weeks of solid darkness lowered ;
What mountain-surges mountain-surges lashed,
What sudden hurricanes the canvas dashed ;
What bursting lightnings, with incessant flare,
Kindled, in one wide flame, the burning air ;
What roaring thunders bellowed o'er our head,

And seemed to shake the reeling ocean's bed:
To tell each horror on the deep revealed,
Would ask an iron throat with tenfold vigor steeled:
Those dreadful wonders of the deep I saw,
Which filled the sailor's breast with sacred awe;
And which the sages, of their learning vain,
Esteem the phantoms of the dreamful brain:
That living fire, by seamen held divine,
Of Heaven's own care in storms the holy sign,
Which, midst the horrors of the tempest plays,
And on the blast's dark wings will gayly blaze;
These eyes distinct have seen that living fire
Glide through the storm, and round my sails aspire.
And oft, while wonder thrilled my breast, mine eyes
To heaven have seen the watery columns rise.
Slender, at first, the subtle fume appears,
And writhing round and round its volume rears;
Thick as a mast the vapor swells its size,
A curling whirlwind lifts it to the skies;
The tube now straightens, now in width extends,
And, in a hovering cloud, its summit ends:
Still, gulp on gulp, in sucks the rising tide,
And now the cloud, with cumbrous weight supplied,
Full-gorged, and blackening, spreads and moves more
        slow,
And, waving, trembles to the waves below.

           *   *   *

    And now, their ensigns blazing o'er the tide,
On India's shore the Lusian heroes ride.
High to the fleecy clouds resplendent far
Appear the regal towers of Malabar,

Imperial Calicut, the lordly seat
Of the first monarch of the Indian state.
Right to the port the valiant Gama bends,
With joyful shouts, a fleet of boats attends:
Joyful, their nets they leave, and finny prey,
And, crowding round the Lusians, point the way.

Luis de Camoens.   Tr. W. J. Mickle.

THE SEA.

THE sea! the sea! the open sea!
   The blue, the fresh, the ever free!
Without a mark, without a bound,
It runneth the earth's wide regions round;
It plays with the clouds; it mocks the skies;
Or like a cradled creature lies.

I 'm on the sea! I 'm on the sea!
I am where I would ever be;
With the blue above, and the blue below,
And silence wheresoe'er I go;
If a storm should come and awake the deep,
What matter? I shall ride and sleep.

I love, oh, how I love to ride
On the fierce, foaming, bursting tide,
When every mad wave drowns the moon,
Or whistles aloft his tempest tune,
And tells how goeth the world below,
And why the sou'west blasts do blow.

I never was on the dull, tame shore,
But I loved the great sea more and more,
And backwards flew to her billowy breast,
Like a bird that seeketh its mother's nest;
And a mother she was, and is, to me;
For I was born on the open sea!

The waves were white, and red the morn,
In the noisy hour when I was born;
And the whale it whistled, the porpoise rolled,
And the dolphins bared their backs of gold;
And never was heard such an outcry wild
As welcomed to life the ocean-child!

I 've lived since then, in calm and strife,
Full fifty summers, a sailor's life,
With wealth to spend and a power to range,
But never have sought nor sighed for change;
And Death, whenever he comes to me,
Shall come on the wild, unbounded sea!

Bryan Waller Procter.

THE STORMY PETREL.

A THOUSAND miles from land are we,
  Tossing about on the roaring sea;
From billow to bounding billow cast,
Like fleecy snow on the stormy blast:
The sails are scattered abroad, like weeds,
The strong masts shake, like quivering reeds,

The mighty cables, and iron chains,
The hull, which all earthly strength disdains,
They strain and they crack, and hearts like stone
Their natural hard, proud strength disown.

Up and down! Up and down!
From the base of the wave to the billow's crown,
And amidst the flashing and feathery foam
The stormy petrel finds a home, —
A home, if such a place may be,
For her who lives on the wide, wide sea,
On the craggy ice, in the frozen air,
And only seeketh her rocky lair
To warm her young, and to teach them to spring
At once o'er the waves on their stormy wing!

O'er the deep! O'er the deep!
Where the whale and the shark and the sword-fish
        sleep,
Outflying the blast and the driving rain,
The Petrel telleth her tale - in vain;
For the mariner curseth the warning bird
Who bringeth him news of the storms unheard!
Ah! thus does the prophet, of good or ill,
Meet hate from the creatures he serveth still;
Yet he never falters. So, Petrel! spring
Once more o'er the waves on thy stormy wing!

Bryan Waller Procter.

THE SEA IN CALM.

LOOK what immortal floods the sunset pours
    Upon us! Mark! how still (as though in dreams
Bound) the once wild and terrible ocean seems!
How silent are the winds! No billow roars:
But all is tranquil as Elysian shores!
The silver margin which aye runneth round
The moon-enchanted sea, hath here no sound;
Even Echo speaks not on these radiant moors!
What! is the giant of the ocean dead,
Whose strength was all unmatched beneath the sun?
No; he reposes! Now his toils are done,
More quiet than the babbling brooks is he.
So mightiest powers by deepest calms are fed,
And sleep, how oft, in things that gentlest be!

Bryan Waller Procter.

THE SEA-SHORE.

METHINKS I fain would lie by the lone sea,
    And hear the waters their white music weave!
Methinks it were a pleasant thing to grieve,
So that our sorrows might companioned be
By that strange harmony
Of winds and billows, and the living sound
Sent down from heaven when the thunder speaks,
Unto the listening shores and torrent creeks,
When the swollen sea doth strive to burst his bound!

Methinks, when tempests come and kiss the ocean,
Until the vast and terrible billows wake,
I see the writhing of that curléd snake,
Which men of old believed, — and my emotion
Warreth within me, till the fable reigns
God of my fancy, and my curdling veins
Do homage to that serpent old,
Which clasped the great world in its fold,
And brooded over earth, and the charmed sea,
Like endless, restless, drear Eternity!

Bryan Walter Procter.

THE OCEAN.

O THOU vast ocean! ever-sounding sea!
  Thou symbol of a drear immensity!
Thou thing that windest round the solid world
Like a huge animal, which, downward hurled
From the black clouds, lies weltering and alone,
Lashing and writhing till its strength be gone!
Thy voice is like the thunder, and thy sleep
Is as a giant's slumber, loud and deep.
Thou speakest in the east and in the west
At once, and on thy heavy-laden breast
Fleets come and go, and things that have no life
Or motion, yet are moved and met in strife.

The earth hath naught of this: no chance nor change
Ruffles its surface, and no spirits dare
Give answer to the tempest-wakened air;
But o'er its wastes the weakly tenants range

At will, and wound its bosom as they go :
Ever the same, it hath no ebb, no flow ;
But in their stated rounds the seasons come,
And pass like visions to their viewless home,
And come again, and vanish : the young Spring
Looks ever bright with leaves and blossoming ;
And Winter always winds his sullen horn,
When the wild Autumn, with a look forlorn
Dies in his strong manhood ; and the skies
Weep, and flowers sicken, when the Summer flies.

Thou only, terrible ocean, hast a power,
A will, a voice, and in thy wrathful hour,
When thou dost lift thine anger to the clouds,
A fearful and magnificent beauty shrouds
Thy broad green forehead. If thy waves be driven
Backward and forward by the shifting wind,
How quickly dost thou thy great strength unbind,
And stretch thine arms, and war at once with Heaven!

Thou trackless and immeasurable main !
On thee no record ever lived again
To meet the hand that writ it ; line nor lead
Hath ever fathomed thy profoundest deeps,
Where haply the huge monster swells and sleeps,
King of his watery limit, who, 't is said,
Can move the mighty ocean into storm, —
O, wonderful thou art, great element,
And fearful in thy spleeny humors bent,
And lovely in repose ; thy summer form
Is beautiful, and when thy silver waves

Make music in earth's dark and winding caves,
I love to wander on thy pebbled beach,
Marking the sunlight at the evening hour,
And hearken to the thoughts thy waters teach, —
"Eternity, Eternity, and Power."

Bryan Waller Procter.

THE OCEAN IN CALM.

IT is the midnight hour; — the beauteous sea,
Calm as the cloudless heaven, the heaven discloses,
While many a sparkling star, in quiet glee,
Far down within the watery sky reposes.
As if the ocean's heart were stirred
With inward life, a sound is heard,
Like that of dreamer murmuring in his sleep;
'T is partly the billow, and partly the air
That lies like a garment floating fair
Above the happy deep.
The sea, I ween, cannot be fanned
By evening freshness from the land,
For the land it is far away;
But God hath willed that the sky-born breeze
In the centre of the loneliest seas
Should ever sport and play.
The mighty moon she sits above,
Encircled with a zone of love,
A zone of dim and tender light
That makes her wakeful eye more bright:
She seems to shine with a sunny ray,

And the night looks like a mellowed day !
The gracious Mistress of the Main
Hath now an undisturbéd reign,
And from her silent throne looks down,
As upon children of her own,
On the waves that lend their gentle breast
In gladness for her couch of rest !

My spirit sleeps amid the calm
The sleep of a new delight;
And hopes that she ne'er may wake again,
But forever hang o'er the lovely main,
And adore the lovely night.
Scarce conscious of an earthly frame,
She glides away like a lambent flame,
And in her bliss she sings ;
Now touching softly the ocean's breast,
Now mid the stars she lies at rest,
As if she sailed on wings!
Now bold as the brightest star that glows
More brightly since at first it rose,
Looks down on the far-off flood,
And there, all breathless and alone,
As the sky where she soars were a world of her own
She mocketh that gentle mighty one
As he lies in his quiet mood.
"Art thou," she breathes, "the tyrant grim
That scoffs at human prayers,
Answering with prouder roar the while,
As it rises from some lonely isle,
Through groans raised wild, the hopeless hymn

Of shipwrecked mariners?
Oh, thou art harmless as a child
Weary with joy, and reconciled
For sleep to change its play;
And now that night hath stayed thy race,
Smiles wander o'er thy placid face
As if thy dreams were gay."

And can it be that for me alone
The main and heavens are spread?
Oh, whither, in this holy hour,
Have those fair creatures fled,
To whom the ocean-plains are given
As clouds possess their native heaven?
The tiniest boat, that ever sailed
Upon an inland lake,
Might through this sea without a fear
Her silent journey take,
Though the helmsman slept as if on land,
And the oar had dropped from the rowers' hand.
How like a monarch would she glide,
While the husht billow kissed her side
With low and lulling tone,
Some stately ship, that from afar
Shone sudden, like a rising star,
With all her bravery on!
List! how in murmurs of delight
The blessed airs of heaven invite
The joyous bark to pass one night
Within their still domain!
O grief! that yonder gentle moon,

Whose smiles forever fade so soon,
Should waste such smiles in vain.
Haste! haste! before the moonshine dies
Dissolved amid the morning skies,
While yet the silvery glory lies
Above the sparkling foam;
Bright mid surrounding brightness, thou,
Scattering fresh beauty from thy prow,
In pomp and splendor come!

And lo! upon the murmuring waves
A glorious shape appearing!
A broad-winged vessel, through the shower
Of glimmering lustre steering!
As if the beauteous ship enjoyed
The beauty of the sea,
She lifteth up her stately head
And saileth joyfully.
A lovely path before her lies,
A lovely path behind;
She sails amid the loveliness
Like a thing with heart and mind.
Fit pilgrim through a scene so fair,
Slowly she beareth on;
A glorious phantom of the deep,
Risen up to meet the moon.
The moon bids her tenderest radiance fall
On her wavy streamer and snow-white wings,
And the quiet voice of the rocking sea
To cheer the gliding vision sings.
Oh, ne'er did sky and water blend

In such a holy sleep,
Or bathe in brighter quietude
A roamer of the deep.
So far the peaceful soul of heaven
Hath settled on the sea,
It seems as if this weight of calm
Were from eternity.
O world of waters! the steadfast earth
Ne'er lay entranced like thee!

John Wilson.

THE RIME OF THE ANCIENT MARINER.

IN SEVEN PARTS

PART I.

IT is an ancient mariner,
  And he stoppeth one of three:
"By thy long gray beard and glittering
    eye,
Now wherefore stopp'st thou me?

"The bridegroom's doors are opened wide,
And I am next of kin;
The guests are met, the feast is set,
Mayst hear the merry din."

He holds him with his skinny hand.
"There was a ship," quoth he.
"Hold off! unhand me, graybeard loon!"
Eftsoons his hand dropt he.

An ancient mariner meeteth three gallants bidden to a wedding feast, and detaineth one

The wedding-guest is spell-bound by the eye of the old seafaring man, and constrained to hear his tale.
He holds him with his glittering eye,
The wedding-guest stood still,
And listens like a three-years' child,
The mariner hath his will.

The wedding-guest sat on a stone,
He cannot choose but hear;
And thus spake on that ancient man,
The bright-eyed mariner :

The ship was cheered, the harbor cleared,
Merrily did we drop
Below the kirk, below the hill,
Below the lighthouse top.

The mariner tells how the ship sailed southward with a good wind and fair weather, till it reached the line.
The sun came up upon the left,
Out of the sea came he !
And he shone bright, and on the right
Went down into the sea.

Higher and higher every day,
Till over the mast at noon —
The wedding-guest here beat his breast,
For he heard the loud bassoon.

The wedding-guest heareth the bridal music; but the mariner continueth his tale.
The bride hath paced into the hall,
Red as a rose is she ;
Nodding their heads before her goes
The merry minstrelsy.

The wedding-guest he beat his breast,
Yet he cannot choose but hear ;

And thus spake on that ancient man,
The bright-eyed mariner :

And now the storm-blast came, and he
Was tyrannous and strong :
He struck with his o'ertaking wings,
And chased us south along.

The ship drawn by a storm toward the south pole

With sloping masts and dripping prow,
As who pursued with yell and blow
Still treads the shadow of his foe,
And forward bends his head,
The ship drove fast, loud roared the blast,
And southward aye we fled.

And now there came both mist and snow,
And it grew wondrous cold ;
And ice, mast-high, came floating by,
As green as emerald.

And through the drifts the snowy clifts
Did send a dismal sheen ·
Nor shapes of men nor beasts we ken
The ice was all between.

The land of ice and of fearful sounds, where no living thing was to be seen

The ice was here, the ice was there,
The ice was all around :
It cracked and growled, and roared and
        howled,
Like noises in a swound !

Till a great sea-bird, called the albatross, came through the snow-fog, and was received with great joy and hospitality.

At length did cross an albatross :
Thorough the fog it came ;
As if it had been a Christian soul,
We hailed it in God's name.

It ate the food it ne'er had eat,
And round and round it flew.
The ice did split with a thunder-fit ;
The helmsman steered us through !

And lo ! the albatross proveth a bird of good omen, and followeth the ship as it returned northward through fog and floating ice.

And a good south-wind sprung up behind ;
The albatross did follow,
And every day, for food or play,
Came to the mariner's hollo !

In mist or cloud, on mast or shroud,
It perched for vespers nine ;
Whiles all the night, through fog-smoke
           white,
Glimmered the white moonshine.

The ancient mariner inhospitably killeth the pious bird of good omen.

" God save thee, ancient mariner !
From the fiends, that plague thee thus !
Why look'st thou so ? " — With my cross-
           bow
I shot the albatross.

PART II.

THE sun now rose upon the right :
Out of the sea came he,
Still hid in mist, and on the left
Went down into the sea.

And the good south-wind still blew behind
But no sweet bird did follow,
Nor any day for food or play
Came to the mariner's hollo!

And I had done an hellish thing,
And it would work 'em woe:
For all averred, I had killed the bird
That made the breeze to blow.
Ah wretch! said they, the bird to slay,
That made the breeze to blow!

His shipmates cry
out against the
ancient mariner,
for killing the
bird of good-luck.

Nor dim nor red, like God's own head,
The glorious sun uprist:
Then all averred, I had killed the bird
That brought the fog and mist.
'Twas right, said they, such birds to slay
That bring the fog and mist.

But when the fog
cleared off, they
justify the same,
and thus make
themselves ac-
complices in the
crime.

The fair breeze blew, the white foam flew,
The furrow followed free;
We were the first that ever burst
Into that silent sea.

The fair breeze
continues, the
ship enters the
Pacific Ocean and
sails northward,
even till it reach-
es the line.

Down dropt the breeze, the sails dropt
    down,
'T was sad as sad could be;
And we did speak only to break
The silence of the sea!

The ship hath
been suddenly
becalmed

All in a hot and copper sky,
The bloody sun, at noon,

Right up above the mast did stand,
No bigger than the moon.

Day after day, day after day,
We stuck, nor breath nor motion;
As idle as a painted ship
Upon a painted ocean.

And the alba-
tross begins to be
avenged.

Water, water, everywhere,
And all the boards did shrink:
Water, water, everywhere,
Nor any drop to drink.

The very deep did rot: O Christ!
That ever this should be!
Yea, slimy things did crawl with legs
Upon the slimy sea.

About, about, in reel and rout
The death-fires danced at night;
The water, like a witch's oils,
Burnt green, and blue and white.

A spirit had fol-
lowed them; one
of the invisible
inhabitants of this
planet, — neither
departed souls
nor angels; con-
cerning whom the learned Jew, Josephus, and the Platonic Constantino-
politan, Michael Psellus, may be consulted. They are very numerous, and
there is no climate or element without one or more.

And some in dreams assuréd were
Of the spirit that plagued us so;
Nine fathom deep he had followed us
From the land of mist and snow.

And every tongue, through utter drought,
Was withered at the root;

We could not speak, no more than if
We had been choked with soot.

Ah! well-a-day! what evil looks
Had I from old and young!
Instead of the cross the albatross
About my neck was hung.

The shipmates, in their sore distress, would fain throw the whole guilt on the ancient mariner; in sign whereof they hang the dead sea-bird round his neck.

PART III.

THERE passed a weary time. Each throat
Was parched, and glazed each eye.
A weary time! a weary time!
How glazed each weary eye,
When looking westward, I beheld
A something in the sky.

The ancient mariner beholdeth a sign in the element afar off

At first it seemed a little speck,
And then it seemed a mist;
It moved and moved, and took at last
A certain shape, I wist.

A speck, a mist, a shape, I wist!
And still it neared and neared.
As if it dodged a water-sprite,
It plunged and tacked and veered.

With throats unslaked, with black lips
baked,
We could nor laugh nor wail;
Through utter drought all dumb we stood;

At its nearer approach, it seemeth him to be a ship; and at a dear ransom he freeth his speech from the bonds of thirst

I bit my arm, I sucked the blood,
And cried, A sail! a sail!

With throats unslaked, with black lips
    baked,
Agape they heard me call;
A flash of joy,   Gramercy! they for joy did grin,
And all at once their breath drew in,
As they were drinking all.

And horror fol-
lows : for can it See! see! (I cried) she tacks no more!
be a ship, that Hither to work us weal;
comes onward
without wind or Without a breeze, without a tide,
tide? She steadies with upright keel!

The western wave was all a flame,
The day was wellnigh done,
Almost upon the western wave
Rested the broad bright sun;
When that strange shape drove suddenly
Betwixt us and the sun.   *r*

It seemeth him
but the skeleton And straight the sun was flecked with bars,
of a ship. (Heaven's Mother send us grace!)
As if through a dungeon-grate he peered
With broad and burning face.

Alas! (thought I, and my heart beat loud)
How fast she nears and nears!
Are those her sails that glance in the sun,
Like restless gossameres?

Are those her ribs through which the sun
Did peer, as through a grate;
And is that woman all her crew?
Is that a Death, and are there two?
Is Death that woman's mate?

And its ribs are seen as bars on the face of the setting sun.

Her lips were red, her looks were free,
Her locks were yellow as gold:
Her skin was as white as leprosy,
The nightmare Life-in-Death was she,
Who thicks man's blood with cold.

The spectre-woman and her death-mate, and no other on board the skeleton-ship, Like vessel, like crew!

The naked hulk alongside came,
And the twain were casting dice;
"The game is done! I've won, I've won!"
Quoth she, and whistles thrice.

Death, and Life-in-Death have diced for the ship's crew, and she (the latter) winneth the ancient mariner.

The sun's rim dips; the stars rush out:
At one stride comes the dark;
With far-heard whisper, o'er the sea
Off shot the spectre-bark.

No twilight within the courts of the sun.

We listened and looked sideways up!
Fear at my heart, as at a cup,
My life-blood seemed to sip!
The stars were dim, and thick the night,
The steersman's face by his lamp gleamed
        white;
From the sails the dew did drip —
Till clomb above the eastern bar
The hornéd moon, with one bright star
Within the nether tip.

At the rising of the moon.

One after an-
other,

One after one, by the star-dogged moon,
Too quick for groan or sigh,
Each turned his face with a ghastly pang,
And cursed me with his eye.

His shipmates
drop down dead.

Four times fifty living men
(And I heard nor sigh nor groan),
With heavy thump, a lifeless lump,
They dropped down one by one.

But Life-in-
Death begins her
work on the an-
cient mariner.

The souls did from their bodies fly, —
They fled to bliss or woe !
And every soul it passed me by
Like the whiz of my cross-bow !

PART IV.

The wedding-
guest feareth that
a spirit is talking
to him ;

"I FEAR thee, ancient mariner !
I fear thy skinny hand !
And thou art long and lank and brown,
As is the ribbed sea-sand.

"I fear thee and thy glittering eye,
And thy skinny hand so brown."

But the ancient
mariner assureth
him of his bodily
life, and proceed-
eth to relate his
horrible penance.

Fear not, fear not, thou wedding-guest !
This body dropt not down.

Alone, alone, all, all alone,
Alone on a wide, wide sea !
And never a saint took pity on
My soul in agony.

The many men, so beautiful!
And they all dead did lie:
And a thousand thousand slimy things
Lived on, and so did I.

He despiseth the creatures of the calm.

I looked upon the rotting sea,
And drew my eyes away;
I looked upon the rotting deck,
And there the dead men lay.

And envieth that they should live, and so many lie dead.

I looked to heaven, and tried to pray;
But or ever a prayer had gushed,
A wicked whisper came, and made
My heart as dry as dust.

I closed my lids, and kept them close,
And the balls like pulses beat;
For the sky and the sea, and the sea and
    the sky,
Lay like a load on my weary eye,
And the dead were at my feet.

The cold sweat melted from their limbs,
Nor rot nor reek did they;
The look with which they looked on me
Had never passed away.

But the curse liveth for him in the eye of the dead men.

An orphan's curse would drag to hell
A spirit from on high,
But oh! more horrible than that
Is a curse in a dead man's eye!

Seven days, seven nights, I saw that
        curse,
And yet I could not die.

In his loneliness
and fixedness he
yearneth towards
the journeying
moon, and the
stars that still so-
journ, yet still
move onward; and everywhere the blue sky belongs to them, and is their
appointed rest, and their native country, and their own natural homes,
which they enter unannounced, as lords that are certainly expected, and
yet there is a silent joy at their arrival.

The moving moon went up the sky,
And nowhere did abide;
Softly she was going up,
And a star or two beside —

Her beams bemocked the sultry main,
Like April hoar-frost spread;
But where the ship's huge shadow lay
The charméd water burnt alway,
A still and awful red.

By the light of
the moon he be-
holdeth God's
creatures of the
great calm.

Beyond the shadow of the ship
I watched the water-snakes:
They moved in tracks of shining white:
And when they reared, the elfish light
Fell off in hoary flakes.

Within the shadow of the ship
I watched their rich attire:
Blue, glossy-green, and velvet-black,
They coiled and swam; and every track
Was a flash of golden fire.

Their beauty and
their happiness.

O happy living things! no tongue
Their beauty might declare:

A spring of love gushed from my heart,
And I blessed them unaware:
Sure my kind saint took pity on me,
And I blessed them unaware.

He blesseth them in his heart.

The selfsame moment I could pray;
And from my neck so free
The albatross fell off, and sank
Like lead into the sea.

The spell begins to break.

PART V.

O SLEEP! it is a gentle thing,
Beloved from pole to pole!
To Mary Queen the praise be given!
She sent the gentle sleep from heaven,
That slid into my soul.

The silly buckets on the deck,
That had so long remained,
I dreamt that they were filled with dew;
And when I awoke, it rained.

By grace of the holy Mother, the ancient mariner is refreshed with rain

My lips were wet, my throat was cold,
My garments all were dank;
Sure I had drunken in my dreams,
And still my body drank.

I moved, and could not feel my limbs:
I was so light — almost
I thought that I had died in sleep,
And was a blesséd ghost.

He heareth
sounds and seeth
strange sights
and commotions
in the sky and
the element.

And soon I heard a roaring wind :
It did not come anear ;
But with its sound it shook the sails,
That were so thin and sere.

The upper air burst into life !
And a hundred fire-flags sheen,
To and fro they were hurried about !
And to and fro, and in and out,
The wan stars danced between.

And the coming wind did roar more loud,
And the sails did sigh like sedge ;
And the rain poured down from one black
     cloud ;
The moon was at its edge.

The thick black cloud was cleft, and still
The moon was at its side :
Like waters shot from some high crag,
The lightning fell with never a jag,
A river steep and wide.

The bodies of the
ship's crew are
inspired, and the
ship moves on ;

The loud wind never reached the ship,
Yet now the ship moved on !
Beneath the lightning and the moon
The dead men gave a groan.

They groaned, they stirred, they all up-
    rose,
Nor spake, nor moved their eyes ;
It had been strange, even in a dream,
To have seen those dead men rise.

The helmsman steered, the ship moved on;
Yet never a breeze up blew;
The mariners all 'gan work the ropes,
Where they were wont to do;
They raised their limbs like lifeless tools, —
We were a ghastly crew.

The body of my brother's son
Stood by me, knee to knee;
The body and I pulled at one rope,
But he said naught to me.

"I fear thee, ancient mariner!"
Be calm, thou wedding-guest!
'T was not those souls that fled in pain,
Which to their corses came again,
But a troop of spirits blest:

For when it dawned — they dropped their
    arms,
And clustered round the mast;
Sweet sounds rose slowly through their
    mouths,
And from their bodies passed

Around, around, flew each sweet sound,
Then darted to the sun;
Slowly the sounds came back again,
Now mixed, now one by one.

Sometimes, a-drooping from the sky,
I heard the skylark sing;

But not by the souls of the men, nor by demons of earth or middle air, but by a blessed troop of angelic spirits, sent down by the invocation of the guardian saint

Sometimes all little birds that are,
How they seemed to fill the sea and air
With their sweet jargoning!

And now 't was like all instruments,
Now like a lonely flute;
And now it is an angel's song,
That makes the heavens be mute.

It ceased; yet still the sails made on
A pleasant noise till noon,
A noise like of a hidden brook
In the leafy month of June,
That to the sleeping woods all night
Singeth a quiet tune.

Till noon we quietly sailed on,
Yet never a breeze did breathe:
Slowly and smoothly went the ship,
Moved onward from beneath.

The lonesome spirit from the south pole carries on the ship as far as the line, in obedience to the angelic troop, but still requireth vengeance.

Under the keel, nine fathom deep,
From the land of mist and snow,
The spirit slid; and it was he
That made the ship to go.
The sails at noon left off their tune,
And the ship stood still also.

The sun, right up above the mast,
Had fixed her to the ocean;
But in a minute she 'gan stir

With a short uneasy motion —
Backwards and forwards half her length
With a short uneasy motion.

Then like a pawing horse let go,
She made a sudden bound:
It flung the blood into my head,
And I fell down in a swound.

How long in that same fit I lay
I have not to declare;
But ere my living life returned,
I heard and in my soul discerned
Two voices in the air:

The polar spirit's fellow-demons, the invisible inhabitants of the element, take part in his wrong; and two of them relate, one to the other, that penance long and heavy for the ancient mariner hath been accorded to the polar spirit, who returneth southward.

"Is it he?" quoth one, "is this the
        man?
By him who died on cross,
With his cruel bow he laid full low
The harmless albatross.

"The spirit who bideth by himself
In the land of mist and snow,
He loved the bird that loved the man
Who shot him with his bow."

The other was a softer voice,
As soft as honey-dew:
Quoth he, "The man hath penance done,
And penance more will do."

PART VI.

FIRST VOICE.

But tell me, tell me! speak again,
Thy soft response renewing —
What makes that ship drive on so fast?
What is the ocean doing?

SECOND VOICE.

Still as a slave before his lord,
The ocean hath no blast;
His great bright eye most silently
Up to the moon is cast —

If he may know which way to go;
For she guides him smooth or grim.
See, brother, see! how graciously
She looketh down on him.

The mariner hath been cast into a trance; for the angelic power causeth the vessel to drive northward faster than human life could endure.

FIRST VOICE.

But why drives on that ship so fast,
Without or wave or wind?

SECOND VOICE.

The air is cut away before,
And closes from behind.

Fly, brother, fly! more high, more high!
Or we shall be belated:
For slow and slow that ship will go,
When the mariner's trance is abated.

I woke, and we were sailing on
As in a gentle weather:
'T was night, calm night, the moon was
   high;
The dead men stood together.

The supernatural motion is retarded; the mariner awakes, and his penance begins anew.

All stood together on the deck,
For a charnel-dungeon fitter:
All fixed on me their stony eyes,
That in the moon did glitter.

The pang, the curse, with which they died,
Had never passed away:
I could not draw my eyes from theirs,
Nor turn them up to pray.

And now this spell was snapt: once more
I viewed the ocean green,
And looked far forth, yet little saw
Of what had else been seen —

The curse is finally expiated.

Like one, that on a lonesome road
Doth walk in fear and dread,
And having once turned round walks on,
And turns no more his head;
Because he knows a frightful fiend
Doth close behind him tread.

But soon there breathed a wind on me,
Nor sound nor motion made:
Its path was not upon the sea,
In ripple or in shade.

It raised my hair, it fanned my cheek
Like a meadow-gale of spring —
It mingled strangely with my fears,
Yet it felt like a welcoming.

Swiftly, swiftly flew the ship,
Yet she sailed softly too :
Sweetly, sweetly blew the breeze —
On me alone it blew.

And the ancient mariner beholdeth his native country.

Oh ! dream of joy ! is this indeed
The lighthouse top I see ?
Is this the hill ? is this the kirk ?
Is this mine own countree ?

We drifted o'er the harbor bar,
And I with sobs did pray —
O let me be awake, my God !
Or let me sleep alway.

The harbor-bay was clear as glass,
So smoothly it was strewn !
And on the bay the moonlight lay,
And the shadow of the moon.

The rock shone bright, the kirk no less
That stands above the rock :
The moonlight steeped in silentness
The steady weathercock.

The angelic spirits leave the dead bodies,

And the bay was white with silent light,
Till, rising from the same,

Full many shapes that shadows were,
In crimson colors came.

A little distance from the prow
Those crimson shadows were:
I turned my eyes upon the deck —
O Christ! what saw I there!

And appear in
their own forms
of light.

Each corse lay flat, lifeless and flat;
And, by the holy rood!
A man all light, a seraph-man,
On every corse there stood.

This seraph band, each waved his hand:
It was a heavenly sight!
They stood as signals to the land,
Each one a lovely light;

This seraph band, each waved his hand,
No voice did they impart —
No voice; but oh! the silence sank
Like music on my heart.

But soon I heard the dash of oars,
I heard the pilot's cheer;
My head was turned perforce away,
And I saw a boat appear.

The pilot and the pilot's boy,
I heard them coming fast:
Dear Lord in heaven! it was a joy
The dead men could not blast.

I saw a third — I heard his voice:
It is the hermit good!
He singeth loud his godly hymns
That he makes in the wood.
He 'll shrive my soul, he 'll wash away
The albatross's blood.

PART VII.

The hermit of
the wood
THIS hermit good lives in that wood
Which slopes down to the sea.
How loudly his sweet voice he rears!
He loves to talk with marineres
That come from a far countrée.

He kneels at morn and noon and eve —
He hath a cushion plump:
It is the moss that wholly hides
The rotted old oak-stump.

The skiff-boat neared; I heard them talk:
"Why, this is strange, I trow!
Where are those lights so many and fair,
That signal made but now?"

Approacheth the
ship with won-
der.
"Strange, by my faith!" the hermit said —
"And they answer not our cheer!
The planks look warped! and see those sails,
How thin they are and sere!
I never saw aught like to them,
Unless perchance it were

"Brown skeletons of leaves that lag
My forest-brook along;
When the ivy-tod is heavy with snow,
And the owlet whoops to the wolf below,
That eats the she-wolf's young."

"Dear Lord! it hath a fiendish look,"
The pilot made reply,
"I am a-feared"—"Push on, push on!"
Said the hermit cheerily.

The boat came closer to the ship,
But I nor spake nor stirred;
The boat came close beneath the ship,
And straight a sound was heard.

Under the water it rumbled on,
Still louder and more dread:
It reached the ship, it split the bay;
The ship went down like lead.

The ship suddenly sinketh.

Stunned by that loud and dreadful sound,
Which sky and ocean smote,
Like one that hath been seven days
        drowned,
My body lay afloat;
But, swift as dreams, myself I found
Within the pilot's boat.

The ancient mariner is saved in the pilot's boat.

Upon the whirl, where sank the ship,
The boat spun round and round;
And all was still, save that the hill
Was telling of the sound.

I moved my lips, — the pilot shrieked,
And fell down in a fit;
The holy hermit raised his eyes,
And prayed where he did sit.

I took the oars : the pilot's boy,
Who now doth crazy go,
Laughed loud and long, and all the while
His eyes went to and fro.
"Ha! ha!" quoth he, "full plain I see,
The Devil knows how to row."

And now, all in my own countree,
I stood on the firm land!
The hermit stepped forth from the boat,
And scarcely he could stand.

The ancient mariner earnestly entreateth the hermit to shrive him; and the penance of life falls on him.

"O, shrive me, shrive me, holy man!"
The hermit crossed his brow.
"Say quick," quoth he, "I bid thee say,
What manner of man art thou?"

Forthwith this frame of mine was wrenched
With a woful agony,
Which forced me to begin my tale;
And then it left me free.

And ever and anon throughout his future life an agony constraineth him to travel from land to land,

Since then, at an uncertain hour,
That agony returns :
And till my ghastly tale is told,
This heart within me burns.

I pass, like night, from land to land;
I have strange power of speech;
That moment that his face I see,
I know the man that must hear me:
To him my tale I teach.

What loud uproar bursts from that door!
The wedding-guests are there:
But in the garden bower the bride
And bridemaids singing are:
And hark! the little vesper bell,
Which biddeth me to prayer!

O wedding-guest! this soul hath been
Alone on a wide wide sea:
So lonely 't was, that God himself
Scarce seemed there to be.

O, sweeter than the marriage-feast,
'T is sweeter far to me,
To walk together to the kirk,
With a goodly company!

To walk together to the kirk,
And all together pray,
While each to his great Father bends,
Old men, and babes, and loving friends,
And youths and maidens gay!

And to teach, by his own example, love and reverence to all things that God made and loveth.

Farewell, farewell! but this I tell
To thee, thou wedding-guest!
He prayeth well who loveth well
Both man and bird and beast.

He prayeth best who loveth best
All things both great and small;
For the dear God who loveth us,
He made and loveth all.

The mariner, whose eye is bright,
Whose beard with age is hoar,
Is gone : and now the wedding-guest
Turned from the bridegroom's door.

He went like one that hath been stunned,
And is of sense forlorn;
A sadder and a wiser man
He rose the morrow morn.

Samuel Taylor Coleridge.

THE FLYING DUTCHMAN.

LONG time ago, from Amsterdam a vessel sailed
away, —
As fair a craft as ever flung aside the laughing spray.
Upon the shore were tearful eyes, and scarfs were in
the air,
As to her, o'er the Zuyder Zee, went fond adieu and
prayer;
And brave hearts, yearning shoreward from the out-
ward-going ship,
Felt lingering kisses clinging still to tear-wet cheek
and lip.
She steered for some far eastern clime, and, as she
skimmed the seas,

Each taper mast was bending like a rod before the
    breeze.

Her captain was a stalwart man, — an iron heart had
    he, —

From childhood's days he lived upon the rolling Zuy-
    der Zee :

He nothing feared upon the earth, scarce heaven itself
    he feared,

He would have dared and done whatever mortal man
    had dared!

He looked aloft, where high in air the pennant cut the
    blue,

And every rope and spar and sail was taut and strong
    and true.

He turned him from the swelling sheet to gaze upon
    the shore, —

Ah! little thought the skipper then 't would meet his
    eye no more ;

He dreamt not that an awful doom was hanging o'er
    his ship,

That Vanderdecken's name would yet make pale the
    speaker's lip.

The vessel bounded on her way, and down and spar
    went down, —

Ere darkness fell, beneath the wave had sunk the dis-
    tant town.

No more, no more, ye hapless crew, shall Holland
    meet your eye.

In lingering hope and keen suspense, maid, wife, and
    child shall die!

Away the brave sea-rover speeds, till sea and sky alone
Are round her, as her course she steers across the tor-
  rid zone.
Away, until the North Star fades, the Southern Cross
  is high,
And myriad gems of brightest beam are sparkling in
  the sky.
The tropic winds are left behind; she nears the Cape
  of Storms,
Where awful Tempest ever sits enthroned in wild
  alarms;
Where Ocean in his anger shakes aloft his foamy
  crest,
Disdainful of the proudest fleets that ride upon his
  breast.
Fierce swells the wind, the rushing wave a deadly chal-
  lenge flings,
And from the wrathful Dutchman's throat a wild defiance rings:
Impotent they to make him swerve, their might he
  dares deride,
And straight he holds his onward course, in the teeth
  of wind and tide.
For days and nights he struggles in the weird, unearthly fight.
His brow is bent, his eye is fierce, but looks of deep
  affright
Amongst the mariners go round, as hopelessly they
  steer:
They do not dare to murmur, but they whisper what
  they fear.

Their black-browed captain awes them: 'neath his darkened eye they quail,
And in a grim and sullen mood their bitter fate bewail.
As some fierce rider ruthless spurs a timid, wavering
   horse,
He drives his shapely vessel, and they watch the reckless course,
Till once again their skipper's laugh is flung upon the
   blast;
The placid ocean smiles beyond, the dreaded Cape is
   passed!

Then northward o'er the Indian main the barque in
   beauty glides;
A thousand murmuring ripples break along her graceful sides:
The perfumed breezes fill her sails, — her destined port
   she nears, —
The captain's brow has lost its frown, the mariners
   their fears.
"Land ho!" at length the welcome sound the watchful sailor sings,
And soon within an Indian bay the ship at anchor
   swings.
Not idle then the busy crew: erelong the spacious hold
Is emptied of its western freight, and stored with silk
   and gold.

Again the ponderous anchor's weighed; the shore is
   left behind,
The snowy sails are bosomed out before the favoring
   wind.

Across the warm blue Indian sea the trader southward
    hies,
And once again the North Star fades and Austral
    beacons rise.
For home she steers! she seems to know and answer
    to the word,
And joyous breasts the dancing wave like some fair
    ocean bird.
"For home! for home!" the merry crew with glad-
    some voices cry,
And e'en the sombre captain has a mild light in his
    eye.

But once again the Cape draws near, and furious surges
    rise;
And still the daring Dutchman's laugh the hurricane
    defies.
But wildly shrieked the tempest ere the scornful sound
    had died,
A warning to the daring man to curb his impious
    pride.
A crested mountain struck the bow, and like a frighted
    bird
She trembled 'neath the awful shock. Then Vander-
    decken heard
A pleading voice within the gale, — his better angel
    spoke,
But fled before his scowling look, as mast-high billows
    broke
O'er deck and poop and bulwark, till the crew with
    terror paled;

But Vanderdecken never flinched, nor 'neath the thun-
    ders quailed.
With folded arms and stern-pressed lips, dark anger in
    his eye,
He answered back the threatening frown that lowered
    o'er the sky.
With fierce impatience in his heart, and scornful look
    of flame,
He spoke, and thus with impious voice blasphemed
    God's holy name : ---
"Howl on, ye winds! ye tempests, howl! your rage is
    spent in vain :
Despite your strength, your frowns, your hate, I'll
    ride upon the main.
Defiance to your idle shrieks! I'll hold my chosen
    path :
I cringe not for thy Maker's smile, — I care not for
    his wrath!"

He ceased. An awful silence fell : the tempest and the
    sea
Were hushed in sudden stillness by the Ruler's dread
    decree.
The ship was riding motionless within the gathering
    gloom ;
The Dutchman stood upon the poop and heard his
    dreadful doom.
The hapless crew were on the deck in swooning ter-
    ror prone,
They, too, were bound in fearful fate. In angered
    thunder-tone

The judgment words swept o'er the sea: "Outcast,
　　arraigned, condemned!　.
Go, toil forever on the deep, by shrieking tempests
　　hemmed.
No home, no port, no calm, no rest, no gentle favor-
　　ing breeze,
Shall ever greet thee.　Go, accurst! and battle with
　　the seas!
Go, braggart! struggle with the storm, nor ever cease
　　to live,
But bear a million times the pangs that death and fear
　　can give.
Away! and hide thy guilty head, a woe to all thy kind
Who ever see thy hopeless strife with ocean and with
　　wind.
Away, presumptuous worm of earth!　Go teach thy
　　fellow-worms
The awful fate that waits on him who braves the King
　　of Storms!"

'T was o'er.　A lurid lightning flash lit up the sea and
　　sky
Around and o'er the fated craft; then rose a wailing cry
From every heart within her, of keen anguish and
　　despair;
But mercy was for them no more, — it died away in
　　air.

Once more the lurid light gleamed out, — the ship was
　　still at rest,
The crew were standing at their posts; with arms
　　across his breast

Still stood the captain on the poop, but bent and
    crouching now

He bowed beneath that fiat dread, and o'er his swarthy
    brow

Swept lines of anguish, as if he a thousand years of
    pain

Had lived and suffered. Then across the heaving,
    sullen main

The tempest shrieked triumphant, and the angry waters
    hissed

Their vengeful hate against the toy they oftentimes had
    kissed.

And ever through the midnight storm that hapless crew
    must speed ;

They try to round the Stormy Cape, but never can suc-
    ceed.

And oft when gales are wildest, and the lightning's
    vivid sheen

Flashes back the ocean's anger, still the Phantom Ship
    is seen

Ever heading to the southward in the fierce tornado's
    swoop,

With her ghostly crew and canvas, and her captain on
    the poop,

Unrelenting, unforgiven ; and 't is said that every word

Of his blasphemous defiance still upon the gale is
    heard !

But heaven help the luckless ones to whom the sight
    appears, -

The doom of those is sealed near whom the ghastly
    sailor steers ;

They 'll never reach their destined port, — they 'll see
    their homes no more, —
They who see the Flying Dutchman — never, never
    reach the shore!

John Boyle O'Reilly.

A LIFE ON THE OCEAN WAVE.

A LIFE on the ocean wave,
    A home on the rolling deep;
Where the scattered waters rave,
    And the winds their revels keep!
Like an eagle caged, I pine
    On this dull, unchanging shore:
Oh! give me the flashing brine,
    The spray and the tempest's roar!

Once more on the deck I stand,
    Of my own swift-gliding craft:
Set sail! farewell to the land!
    The gale follows fair abaft.
We shoot through the sparkling foam
    Like an ocean-bird set free; —
Like the ocean-bird, our home
    We 'll find far out on the sea.

The land is no longer in view,
    The clouds have begun to frown;
But with a stout vessel and crew,
    We 'll say, Let the storm come down!

And the song of our hearts shall be,
  While the winds and the waters rave,
A home on the rolling sea!
  A life on the ocean wave!

Epes Sargent.

NIGHT AT SEA.

THE lovely purple of the noon's bestowing
  Has vanished from the waters, where it flung
A royal color, such as gems are throwing
  Tyrian or regal garniture among.
'T is night, and overhead the sky is gleaming,
  Through the slight vapor trembles each dim star;
I turn away — my heart is sadly dreaming
  Of scenes they do not light, of scenes afar.
    My friends, my absent friends!
      Do you think of me, as I think of you?

By each dark wave around the vessel sweeping,
  Farther am I from old dear friends removed;
Till the lone vigil that I now am keeping,
  I did not know how much you were beloved.
How many acts of kindness little heeded,
  Kind looks, kind words, rise half reproachful now!
Hurried and anxious, my vexed life has speeded,
  And memory wears a soft accusing brow.
    My friends, my absent friends!
      Do you think of me, as I think of you?

The very stars are strangers, as I catch them
  Athwart the shadowy sails that swell above;

I cannot hope that other eyes will watch them
  At the same moment with a mutual love.
They shine not there, as here they now are shining;
  The very hours are changed. — Ah, do ye sleep?
O'er each home pillow midnight is declining —
  May some kind dream at least my image keep!
    My friends, my absent friends!
      Do you think of me, as I think of you?

Yesterday has a charm, To-day could never
  Fling o'er the mind, which knows not till it parts
How it turns back with tenderest endeavor
  To fix the past within the heart of hearts.
Absence is full of memory, it teaches
  The value of all old familiar things;
The strengthener of affection, while it reaches
  O'er the dark parting, with an angel's wings.
    My friends, my absent friends!
      Do you think of me, as I think of you?

The world, with one vast element omitted —
  Man's own especial element, the earth;
Yet, o'er the waters is his rule transmitted
  By that great knowledge whence has power its birth.
How oft on some strange loveliness while gazing,
  Have I wished for you — beautiful as new,
The purple waves like some wild army raising
  Their snowy banners as the ship cuts through.
    My friends, my absent friends!
      Do you think of me, as I think of you?

Bearing upon its wings the hues of morning,
  Up springs the flying-fish like life's false joy,
Which of the sunshine asks that frail adorning
  Whose very light is fated to destroy.
Ah, so doth genius on its rainbow pinion
  Spring from the depths of an unkindly world;
So spring sweet fancies from the heart's dominion —
  Too soon in death the scorched-up wing is furled.
    My friends, my absent friends!
      Whate'er I see is linked with thoughts of you.

No life is in the air, but in the waters
  Are creatures, huge and terrible and strong;
The swordfish and the shark pursue their slaughters,
  War universal reigns these depths along.
Like some new island in the ocean springing,
  Floats on the surface some gigantic whale,
From its vast head a silver fountain flinging,
  Bright as the fountain in a fairy tale.
    My friends, my absent friends!
      I read such fairy legends while with you.

Light is amid the gloomy canvas spreading,
  The moon is whitening the dusky sails,
From the thick bank of clouds she masters, shedding
  The softest influence that o'er night prevails.
Pale is she like a young queen pale with splendor,
  Haunted with passionate thoughts too fond, too deep;
The very glory that she wears is tender,
  The very eyes that watch her beauty fain would
    weep.

My friends, my absent friends!
    Do you think of me, as I think of you?

Sunshine is ever cheerful, when the morning
    Wakens the world with cloud-dispelling eyes;
The spirits mount to glad endeavor, scorning
    What toil upon a path so sunny lies.
Sunshine and hope are comrades, and their weather
    Calls into life an energy like Spring's;
But memory and moonlight go together,
    Reflected in the light that either brings.
        My friends, my absent friends!
            Do you think of me, then?   I think of you.

The busy deck is hushed, no sounds are waking
    But the watch pacing silently and slow;
The waves against the sides incessant breaking,
    And rope and canvas swaying to and fro.
The topmast sail, it seems like some dim pinnacle
    Cresting a shadowy tower amid the air;
While red and fitful gleams come from the binnacle,
    The only light on board to guide us — where?
        My friends, my absent friends!
            Far from my native land, and far from you.

On one side of the ship, the moonbeam's shimmer
    In luminous vibrations sweeps the sea,
But where the shadow falls, a strange, pale glimmer
    Seems, glowworm like, amid the waves to be.
All that the spirit keeps of thought and feeling
    Takes visionary hues from such an hour;

But while some fantasy is o'er me stealing,
  I start — remembrance has a keener power:
    My friends, my absent friends!
      From the fair dream I start to think of you.

A dusk line in the moonlight — I discover
  What all day long I vainly sought to catch;
Or is it but the varying clouds that hover
  Thick in the air, to mock the eyes that watch?
No; well the sailor knows each speck, appearing,
  Upon the tossing waves, the far-off strand;
To that dark line our eager ship is steering.
  Her voyage done — to-morrow we shall land.

Letitia Elizabeth Landon.

A HYMN OF THE SEA.

THE sea is mighty, but a mightier sways
  His restless billows. Thou, whose hands have
    scooped
His boundless gulfs and built his shore, thy breath,
That moved, in the beginning o'er his face,
Moves o'er it evermore. The obedient waves
To its strong motion roll, and rise and fall.
Still from that realm of rain thy cloud goes up,
As at the first, to water the great earth,
And keep her valleys green. A hundred realms
Watch its broad shadow warping on the wind,
And in the dropping shower with gladness hear
Thy promise of the harvest. I look forth

Over the boundless blue, where joyously
The bright crests of innumerable waves
Glance to the sun at once, as when the hands
Of a great multitude are upward flung
In acclamation. I behold the ships
Gliding from cape to cape, from isle to isle,
Or stemming toward far lands, or hastening home
From the Old World. It is thy friendly breeze
That bears them, with the riches of the land,
And treasure of dear lives, till, in the port,
The shouting seaman climbs and furls the sail.

But who shall bide thy tempest, who shall face
The blast that wakes the fury of the sea?
O God! thy justice makes the world turn pale,
When on the armed fleet, that royally
Bears down the surges, carrying war, to smite
Some city, or invade some thoughtless realm,
Descends the fierce tornado. The vast hulks
Are whirled like chaff upon the waves; the sails
Fly, rent like webs of gossamer; the masts
Are snapped asunder; downward from the decks,
Downward are slung, into the fathomless gulf,
Their cruel engines; and their hosts, arrayed
In trappings of the battle-field, are whelmed
By whirlpools, or dashed dead upon the rocks.
Then stand the nations still with awe, and pause
A moment from the bloody work of war.

These restless surges eat away the shores
Of earth's old continents; the fertile plain

Welters in shallows, headlands crumble down,
And the tide drifts the sea-sand in the streets
Of the drowned city. Thou, meanwhile, afar
In the green chambers of the middle sea,
Where broadest spread the waters, and the line
Sinks deepest, while no eye beholds thy work,
Creator! thou dost teach the coral worm
To lay his mighty reefs. From age to age
He builds beneath the waters, till, at last,
His bulwarks overtop the brine, and check
The long wave rolling from the southern pole
To break upon Japan. Thou bidd'st the fires,
That smoulder under ocean, heave on high
The new-made mountains, and uplift their peaks,
A place of refuge for the storm-driven bird.
The birds and wafting billows plant the rifts
With herb and tree; sweet fountains gush; sweet airs
Ripple the living lakes that, fringed with flowers,
Are gathered in the hollows. Thou dost look
On thy creation, and pronounce it good.
Its valleys, glorious with their summer green,
Praise thee in silent beauty, and its woods,
·Swept by the murmuring winds of ocean, join
The murmuring shores in a perpetual hymn.

William Cullen Bryant.

THE SHIPWRECK.

BUT list! a low and moaning sound
At distance heard, like a spirit's song,
And now it reigns above, around.

As if it called the ship along.
The moon is sunk; and a clouded gray
Declares that her course is run,
And, like a god who brings the day,
Up mounts the glorious sun.
Soon as his light has warmed the seas,
From the parting cloud fresh blows the breeze;
And that is the spirit whose well-known song
Makes the vessel to sail in joy along.
No fears hath she; — her giant form
O'er wrathful surge, through blackening storm,
Majestically calm would go
Mid the deep darkness white as snow!
But gently now the small waves glide
Like playful lambs o'er a mountain's side.
So stately her bearing, so proud her array,
The main she will traverse for ever and aye.
Many ports will exult at the gleam of her mast! —
Hush! hush! thou vain dreamer! this hour is her last.
Five hundred souls in one instant of dread
Are hurried o'er the deck;
And fast the miserable ship
Becomes a lifeless wreck.
Her keel hath struck on a hidden rock,
Her planks are torn asunder,
And down come her masts with a reeling shock,
And a hideous crash like thunder.
Her sails are draggled in the brine
That gladdened late the skies,
And her pendant that kissed the fair moonshine
Down many a fathom lies.

Her beauteous sides, whose rainbow hues
Gleamed softly from below,
And flung a warm and sunny flush
O'er the wreaths of murmuring snow,
To the coral rocks are hurrying down
To sleep amid colors as bright as their own.

O, many a dream was in the ship
An hour before her death;
And sights of home with sighs disturbed
The sleepers' long-drawn breath.
Instead of the murmur of the sea
The sailor heard the humming tree
Alive through all its leaves,
The hum of the spreading sycamore
That grows before his cottage-door,
And the swallow's song in the eaves.
His arms enclosed a blooming boy,
Who listened with tears of sorrow and joy
To the dangers his father had passed;
And his wife, - by turns she wept and smiled,
As she looked on the father of her child
Returned to her heart at last.
He wakes at the vessel's sudden roll,
And the rush of waters is in his soul.
Astounded the reeling deck he paces,
Mid hurrying forms and ghastly faces; —
The whole ship's crew are there!
Wailings around and overhead,
Brave spirits stupefied or dead,
And madness and despair.

Leave not the wreck, thou cruel boat!
While yet 't is thine to save,
And angel-hands will bid thee float
Uninjured o'er the wave,
Though whirlpools yawn across thy way,
And storms, impatient for their prey,
Around thee fiercely rave!
Vain all the prayers of pleading eyes,
Of outcry loud and humble sighs,
Hands clasped, or wildly tossed on high
To bless or curse in agony!
Despair and resignation vain!
Away like a strong-winged bird she flies,
That heeds not human miseries,
And far off in the sunshine dies
Like a wave of the restless main!
Hush! hush! Ye wretches left behind!
Silence becomes the brave, resigned
To unexpected doom.

           *   *   *

Now is the ocean's bosom bare,
Unbroken as the floating air;
The ship hath melted quite away,
Like a struggling dream at break of day.
No image meets my wandering eye
But the new-risen sun, and the sunny sky.
Though the night-shades are gone, yet a vapor dull
Bedims the waves so beautiful;
While a low and melancholy moan
Mourns for the glory that hath flown.

John Wilson.

THE SHIPWRECK.

'TWAS twilight, for the sunless day went down
   Over the waste of waters; like a veil,
Which, if withdrawn, would but disclose the frown
   Of one who hates us, so the night was shown,
And grimly darkled o'er their faces pale,
   And hopeless eyes, which o'er the deep alone
Gazed dim and desolate; twelve days had Fear
Been their familiar, and now Death was here.

      *   *   *

At half past eight o'clock, booms, hencoops, spars,
   And all things, for a chance, had been cast loose,
That still could keep afloat the struggling tars,
   For yet they strove, although of no great use:
There was no light in heaven but a few stars,
   The boats put off o'ercrowded with their crews;
She gave a heel, and then a lurch to port,
And, going down head foremost,   sunk, in short.

Then rose from sea to sky the wild farewell!
   Then shrieked the timid, and stood still the brave;
Then some leaped overboard with dreadful yell,
   As eager to anticipate their grave;
And the sea yawned around her like a hell,
   And down she sucked with her the whirling wave,
Like one who grapples with his enemy,
And strives to strangle him before he die.

And first one universal shriek there rushed,
   Louder than the loud ocean, like a crash
Of echoing thunder; and then all was hushed,
   Save the wild wind and the remorseless dash
Of billows; but at intervals there gushed,
   Accompanied with a convulsive splash,
A solitary shriek — the bubbling cry
Of some strong swimmer in his agony.

Lord Byron.

THE WATER-SPOUT.

O'ER the smooth bosom of the faithless tides,
  Propelled by flattering gales, the vessel glides:
Rodmond, exulting, felt the auspicious wind,
And by a mystic charm its aim confined.
The thoughts of home that o'er his fancy roll,
With trembling joy dilate Palemon's soul;
Hope lifts his heart, before whose vivid ray
Distress recedes, and danger melts away.
Tall Ida's summit now more distant grew,
And Jove's high hill was rising to the view;
When on the larboard quarter they descry
A liquid column towering shoot on high;
The foaming base the angry whirlwinds sweep,
Where curling billows rouse the fearful deep:
Still round and round the fluid vortex flies,
Diffusing briny vapors o'er the skies.
This vast phenomenon, whose lofty head,
In heaven immersed, embracing clouds o'erspread.

In spiral motion first, as seamen deem,
Swells, when the raging whirlwind sweeps the stream.
The swift volution, and the enormous train,
Let sages versed in nature's lore explain.
The horrid apparition still draws nigh,
And white with foam the whirling billows fly.
The guns were primed; the vessel northward veers,
Till her black battery on the column bears:
The nitre fired, and, while the dreadful sound
Convulsive shook the slumbering air around,
The watery volume, trembling to the sky,
Burst down, a dreadful deluge, from on high!
The expanding ocean trembled as it fell,
And felt with swift recoil her surges swell;
But soon, this transient undulation o'er,
The sea subsides, the whirlwinds rage no more.
While southward now the increasing breezes veer,
Dark clouds incumbent on their wings appear;
Ahead they see the consecrated grove
Of Cyprus, sacred once to Cretan Jove.
The ship beneath her lofty pressure reels,
And to the freshening gale still deeper heels.

William Falconer.

SIR HUMPHREY GILBERT.

SOUTHWARD with fleet of ice
Sailed the corsair Death;
Wild and fast blew the blast,
And the east-wind was his breath.

His lordly ships of ice
  Glisten in the sun;
On each side, like pennons wide,
  Flashing crystal streamlets run.

His sails of white sea-mist
  Dripped with silver rain;
But where he passed there were cast
  Leaden shadows o'er the main.

Eastward from Campobello
  Sir Humphrey Gilbert sailed;
Three days or more seaward he bore,
  Then, alas! the land-wind failed.

Alas! the land-wind failed,
  And ice-cold grew the night;
And nevermore, on sea or shore,
  Should Sir Humphrey see the light.

He sat upon the deck,
  The Book was in his hand;
" Do not fear! Heaven is as near,"
  He said, " by water as by land!"

In the first watch of the night,
  Without a signal's sound,
Out of the sea, mysteriously,
  The fleet of Death rose all around.

The moon and the evening star
  Were hanging in the shrouds;

Every mast, as it passed,
  Seemed to rake the passing clouds.

They grappled with their prize,
  At midnight black and cold!
As of a rock was the shock;
  Heavily the ground-swell rolled.

Southward through day and dark,
  They drift in close embrace,
With mist and rain, o'er the open main;
  Yet there seems no change of place.

Southward, forever southward,
  They drift through dark and day;
And like a dream, in the Gulf Stream
  Sinking, vanish all away.

Henry Wadsworth Longfellow.

KANE.

DIED FEBRUARY 16, 1857.

ALOFT upon an old basaltic crag,
  Which, sculped by kern winds that defend the Pole,
  Gazes with dead face on the seas that roll
Around the secret of the mystic zone,
A mighty nation's star-bespangled flag
      Flutters alone.
And underneath, upon the lifeless front
  Of that drear cliff a simple name is traced;
Fit type of him who, famishing and gaunt,

But with a rocky purpose in his soul,
    Breasted the gathering snows,
    Clung to the drifting floes,
By want beleaguered, and by winter chased,
Seeking the brother lost amid that frozen waste.

Not many months ago we greeted him,
    Crowned with the icy honors of the North,
    Across the land his hard-won fame went forth,
And Maine's deep woods were shaken limb by limb.
    His own mild Keystone State, sedate and prim,
    Burst from decorous quiet as he came.
    Hot Southern lips, with eloquence aflame,
Sounded his triumph. Texas, wild and grim,
Proffered its horny hand. The large-lunged West,
    From out his giant breast,
Yelled its frank welcome. And from main to main,
    Jubilant to the sky,
    Thundered the mighty cry,
    Honor to Kane!

In vain, — in vain beneath his feet we flung
    The reddening roses! All in vain we poured
    The golden wine, and round the shining board
Sent the toast circling, till the rafters rung
    With the thrice-tripled honors of the feast!
    Scarce the buds wilted and the voices ceased
Ere the pure light that sparkled in his eyes,
Bright as auroral fires in Southern skies,
    Faded and faded! And the brave young heart
That the relentless Arctic winds had robbed

Of all its vital heat, in that long quest
For the lost captain, now within his breast
 More and more faintly throbbed.
His was the victory; but as his grasp
Closed on the laurel crown with eager clasp,
   Death launched a whistling dart;
And ere the thunders of applause were done
His bright eyes closed forever on the sun!
Too late, — too late the splendid prize he won
In the Olympic race of Science and of Art!
Like to some shattered berg that, pale and lone,
Drifts from the white North to a Tropic zone,
   And in the burning day
   Wastes peak by peak away,
   Till on some rosy even
It dies with sunlight blessing it; so he
Tranquilly floated to a Southern sea,
   And melted into heaven!

He needs no tears who lived a noble life!
 We will not weep for him who died so well;
 But we will gather round the hearth, and tell
   The story of his strife:
   Such homage suits him well,
Better than funeral pomp or passing bell!

What tale of peril and self-sacrifice!
Prisoned amid the fastnesses of ice,
 With hunger howling o'er the wastes of snow!
 Night lengthening into months; the ravenous floe
Crunching the massive ships, as the white bear

Crunches his prey. The insufficient share
    Of loathsome food;
The lethargy of famine; the despair
    Urging to labor, nervelessly pursued;
    Toil done with skinny arms, and faces hued
Like pallid masks, while dolefully behind
Glimmered the fading embers of a mind!
That awful hour, when through the prostrate band
Delirium stalked, laying his burning hand
    Upon the ghastly foreheads of the crew;
    The whispers of rebellion, faint and few
    At first, but deepening ever till they grew
Into black thoughts of murder, — such the throng
Of horrors bound the hero. High the song
Should be that hymns the noble part he played!
Sinking himself, yet ministering aid
    To all around him. By a mighty will
    Living defiant of the wants that kill,
Because his death would seal his comrades' fate;
    Cheering with ceaseless and inventive skill
Those polar waters, dark and desolate.
Equal to every trial, every fate,
    He stands, until spring, tardy with relief,
        Unlocks the icy gate,
And the pale prisoners thread the world once more
To the steep cliffs of Greenland's pastoral shore
    Bearing their dying chief!

Time was when he should gain his spurs of gold
    From royal hands, who wooed the knightly state;
The knell of old formalities is tolled,

And the world's knights are now self-consecrate.
No grander episode doth chivalry hold
  In all its annals, back to Charlemagne,
  Than that lone vigil of unceasing pain,
Faithfully kept through hunger and through cold,
  By the good Christian knight, Elisha Kane!

Fitz-James O'Brien.

REEFING TOPSAILS.

A NOBLE sport and my delight —
That reefing topsails! just to make all right,
Ere the wind freshens to a gale at night.
See! clambering nimbly up the shrouds,
Go, thick as bees, the sailor-crowds;
The smartest for the post of honor vie
That weather yard-arm pointing to the sky:
  They gather at the topmast-head,
  And dark against the darkling cloud
  Sidling along the foot-ropes spread;
  Dim figures o'er the yard-arm bowed,
How with the furious sail, a glorious sight,
Up in the darkness of the sky they fight!
  While by the fierce encounter troubled
The heavy pitching of the ship is doubled;
The big sail's swelling, surging volumes, full
Of wind, the strong reef-tackle half restrains;
  And like some lasso-tangled bull
Checked in its mid career of savage might
  O'er far La Plata's plains,
It raves and tugs and plunges to get free,

And flaps and bellows in its agony!
But slowly yielding to its scarce-seen foes
Faint and more faint its frenzied struggling grows;
    Till, by its frantic rage at length
Exhausted, like that desert-ranger's strength,
Silent and still, it seems to shrink and close;
Then, tight comprest, the reef-points firmly tied,
Down to the deck again the sailors glide;
And easier now, with calm concentred force,
The ship bounds forward on her lightened course.
                    Alfred Domett.

THE SHIPWRECK.

IN deep blue sky the sun is bright;
  The port some few miles off in sight;
The pleasant sea's subsiding swell
Of gales for days gone by may tell,
But on the bar no breaker white,
Only as yet a heavier roll
Denotes where lurks that dangerous shoal.
Alert with lead and chart and glass,
The pilot seeks the well-known pass;
All his familiar marks in view
Together brought, distinct and true.
Erelong the tide's decreasing stream
Chafes at the nearer bank beneath;
The sea's dark face begins to gleam
(Like tiger roused that shows his teeth)
With many a white foam-streak and seam:
Still should the passage, though more rough,

Have depth of water, width enough.
But why, though fair the wind and filled
The sails, though masts and cordage strain,
Why hangs, as by enchantment stilled,
The ship unmoving? All in vain
The helm is forced hard down; 't is plain
The shoal has shifted, and the ship
Has touched, but o'er its tail, may slip:
She strains, — she moves, — a moment's bound,
She makes ahead, — then strikes again
With greater force the harder ground.
She broaches to, her broadside black
Full in the breakers' headlong track;
They leap like tigers on their prey;
She rolls as on they come amain,
Rolls heavily as in writhing pain.
The precious time flies fast away, —
The launch is swiftly planned and sent
Over the lee, with wild intent
To anchor grapplings where the tide
Runs smoother, and the ship might ride
Secure beyond the raging bar,
Could they but haul her off so far.
The boat against her bows is smashed;
Beneath the savage surges dashed,
Sucked under by the reflowent wave,
They vanish, all those seamen brave.
On, on, — the breakers press, — no check,
No pause, — fly hissing o'er the wreck,
And scour along the dangerous deck.
The bulwarks on the seaward side,

Boats, rudder, stern-post iron-tied
With deep-driven bolts, — how vain a stay!
The weight of waters tears away.
Alas! and nothing can be done, —
No downward-hoisted flag, no gun
Be got at to give greater stress
To that unheard demand for aid
By the lost ship's whole aspect made, —
Herself, in piteous helplessness,
One huge sad signal of distress.
Still on and on, the tide's return
Redoubling now their rage and bulk,
In one fierce sweep from stem to stern
The thundering sheets of breakers roar,
High as the tops in spray-clouds soar,
And down in crashing cataracts pour
Over the rolling tortured hulk.
Death glares in every horrid shape, —
No help, no mercy, no escape!
For falling spars dash out the brains
Of some, and flying guns adrift,
Or splinters crush them, — slaughter swift
Whereof no slightest trace remains,
The furious foam no bloodshed stains:
Up to the yards and tops they go, —
No hope, no chance of life below!
Then as each ponderous groaning mast
Rocks loosened from its hold at last,
The shrouds and stays, now hanging slack,
Now jerking, bounding tensely back,
Fling off the helpless victims fast,

Like refuse on the yeast of death
That bellows, raves, and boils beneath.
One hapless wretch around his waist
A knotted rope has loosely braced;
When from the stay to which he clings
The jerking mast the doomed one flings,
It slips, and by the neck he swings:
Death grins and glares in hideous shape, —
No hope, no pity, no escape!
Still on and on, all day the same,
Through all that brilliant summer day
Beneath a sky so blithe and blue
The wild white whirl of waters flew,
In stunning volleys overswept
And beat the black ship's yielding frame,
And all around roared, tossed, and leapt
Mad-wreathing swathes of snow! affray
More dire than most disastrous rout
Of some conceivable array
Of thronged white elephants, — as they
Their phalanx broke in warfare waged
In Siam or the Punjaub, — raged
And writhed their great white trunks about,
With screams that shrill as trumpets rung,
And drove destruction everywhere
In maddened terror at the shout
Of turbaned hosts and torches' flare
Full in their monstrous faces flung; —
Wide horror! but to this, no less,
This furious lashing wilderness,
Innocuous-seeming, transient, tame!

Still on, still on, like fiends of Hell
Whiter than angels, frantic, fell,
Through all that summer day the same
The merciless murderous breakers came,
And to the mizzen-top that swayed
With every breach those breakers made,
Unaided, impotent to aid,
The mates and master clung all day.
There, while the sun onlooking gay
Triumphant trod his bright highway, —
There, till his cloudless rich decline,
Faint in the blinding deafening drench
Of salt waves roaring down the whine
And creaking groans each grinding wrench
Took from the tortured timbers, — there
All day, all day, in their despair,
The gently brave, the roughly good,
Collected, calm and silent stood.
That hideous doom they firmly face ;
To no unmanly moans give way,
No frantic gestures; none disgrace
With wild bravado, vain display,
Their end, but like true men await
The dread extremity of fate.
Alas ! and yet no tongue can tell
What thoughts of life and loved ones swell
With anguish irrepressible,
The hearts these horrors fail to quell.
The master urges them to prayer,
"No hope on earth, be heaven your care ! "
And is it mockery — Oh, but mark

Those masts and crowding figures, dark
Against the flush of love and rest
Suffusing all the gorgeous west
In tearful golden glory drest, —
Such soft majestic tenderness,
As of a power that longs to bless
With ardors of divinest breath
All but one raging spot of death;
For all the wide expanse beside
Is blushing, beauteous as a bride,
And a fierce wedding-day indeed
It seems, of Life and Death, with none to heed.

And now the foam spurts up between
The starting deck-planks; downward bowed
The mighty masts terrific lean;
Then each with its despairing crowd
Of life, with one tremendous roar
Falls like a tower, --and all is o'er.

Alfred Domett

THE SOUTHERN CROSS.

WHENE'ER those southern seas I sail,
I find my eyes instinctive° turning
Where, pure and marvellously pale,
Four sacred stars are brightly burning.

A star is set above the thorns;
Two mark the bleeding palms extended;
And one the wounded feet adorns, --
In four the potent cross is blended.

One only hand had power to place
  The symbol there, and that immortal;
Those fair, celestial fires may grace
  And beautify the heavenly portal.

Whatever danger I may meet
  . Upon the wild, disastrous ocean,
Still turn my trusting eyes to greet
  That flaming cross with true devotion.

Nor cease, my willing heart, to give
  Thy prayers and every just endeavor;
For only by the cross I live,
  And by the cross I live forever.

                    Charles Warren Stoddard.

APPENDIX.

Bermudas.

BERMOOTHES.

UNDER the eaves of a Southern sky,
　　Where the cloud-roof bends to the ocean-floor,
Hid in lonely seas, the Bermoothes lie, —
　　An emerald cluster that Neptune bore
Away from the covetous earth-gods' sight,
And placed in a setting of sapphire light.

Prospero's realm, and Miranda's isles,
　　Floating to music of Ariel
Upon fantasy's billow, that glows and smiles
　　Flushing response to the lovely spell, —
Tremulous color and outline seem
Lucent as glassed in a life-like dream.

And away and afar as in dreams we drift
　　Glimmer the blossoming orange groves;
And the dolphin-tints of the waters shift,
　　And the angel-fish through the pure lymph moves

Like the gleam of a rainbow; and soft clouds sweep
Over isle and wave like the wings of sleep.

Deepens the dream into memory now:
　　The straight roads cut through the cedar hills,
The coral cliffs, and the roofs of snow,
　　And the crested cardinal-bird, that trills
A carol clear as the ripple of red
He made in the air as he flashed overhead.

Through pathways trodden of many feet
　　The gray little ground-dove follows and cooes;
Yonder blue-throat stirs to a ballad sweet
　　As ever was mingled with Northern dews;
And the boatswain-bird from the calm lagoon
Lifts his white length into cloudless noon.

See the banana's broad pennons the wind
　　Has torn into shreds in his tropical mood!
Look at the mighty old tamarind,
　　That bore fruit in Saladin's babyhood:
See the pomegranates begin to burn,
And the roses, roses, at every turn!

Into high calms of the sunny air
　　The aloe climbs with her golden flower,
While sentinel yucca and prickly-pear
　　With lance and with bayonet guard her bower,
And the life-leaf creeps by its fibred edge
To hang out gay bells from the jutting ledge.

A glory of oleander bloom
  Borders every bend of the craggy road ;
Lemon and spice trees with rare perfume
  Lingering cloud-fleets heavily load ;
And over the beauty and over the balm
Rises the crown of the royal palm.

Far into the hillside's caverns wind :
  Pillar and ceiling of stalactite
Mirrored in lakes the red torches find ;
  Corridors zigzag from light to light :
And the long fern swings down the slippery stair
Over thresholds curtained with maiden-hair.

Outside, with a motion weirdly slow,
  The mangrove walks through secluded coves,
Leaning on crutch-like boughs, that grow
  To a rooted network of thickets and groves,
Where, sheltered by jagged rock-shelves wide,
Eeriest sprites of the deep might hide.

Under this headland cliff as you row,
  Follow its bastioned layers down
Into fathomless crystal far below
  Vision or ken : spite of old renown,
So massive a wall could Titan erect
As the little coralline architect ?

Against the dusk arches of surf-worn caves,
  In a shimmer of beryl eddies the tide,
Or brightens to topaz where the waves
  Outlined in foam on the reef subside,

Or shades into delicate opaline bands
Dreamily lapsing on pale pink sands.

Wherever you wander the sea is in sight,
　　With its changeable turquoise green and blue,
And its strange transparence of limpid light.
　　You can watch the work that the Nereids do,
Down, down, where their purple fans unfurl,
Planting their coral and sowing their pearl.

Who knows the spot where Atlantis sank?
　　Myths of a lovely drowned continent
Homeless drift over waters blank:
　　What if these reefs were her monument?
Isthmus and cavernous cape may be
Her mountain-summits escaped from the sea.

Spirits alone in these islands dwelt
　　All the dumb, dim years ere Columbus sailed,
The old voyagers said; and it might be spelt
　　Into dream-book of legend, if wonders failed,
They were demons that shipwrecked Atlantis, affrayed
At the terror of silence themselves had made.

Whatever their burthen, the winds have a sound
　　As of muffled voices that, sighing, bewail
An unchronicled sorrow, around and around
　　Whispering and hushing a half-told tale,—
A musical mystery, filling the air
With its endless pathos of vague despair.

And again into fantasy's billowy play
　　Ripples memory back with elusive change;

For chrysolite oceans, a blank of gray,
　　Fringed with the films of a mirage strange, —
A shimmering blur of blossom and gleam :
Can it be Bermoothes ? or is it a dream ?

Lucy Larcom.

———◦◦◦———

New Zealand.

NEW ZEALAND SCENERY.

IT was a wondrous realm beguiled
　Our youth amid its charms to roam;
O'er scenes more fair, serenely wild,
·Not often summer's glory smiled ;
When flecks of cloud, transparent, bright
No alabaster half so white
Hung lightly in a luminous dome
Of sapphire --seemed to float and sleep
Far in the front of its blue steep ;
And almost awful, none the less
For its liquescent loveliness.
Behind them sunk　just o'er the hill —
The deep abyss, profound and still,
The so immediate Infinite,
That yet emerged, the same, it seemed
In hue divine and melting balm,
In many a lake whose crystal calm
Uncrisped, unwrinkled, scarcely gleamed :

Where sky above and lake below
Would like one sphere of azure show,
Save for the circling belt alone,
The softly painted purple zone
Of mountains, bathed where nearer seen
In sunny tints of sober green,
With velvet dark of woods between,
All glossy glooms and shifting sheen;
While here and there some peak of snow
Would o'er their tenderer violet lean.

And yet within this region, fair
With wealth of waving woods, — these glades
And glens and lustre-smitten shades,
Where trees of tropic beauty rare
With graceful spread and ample swell
Uprose, — and that strange asphodel
On tufts of stiff green bayonet-blades,
Great bunches of white bloom upbore,
Like blocks of sea-washed madrepore,
That steeped the noon in fragrance wide,
Till, by the exceeding sweet opprest,
The stately tree-fern leaned aside
For languor, with its starry crown
Of radiating fretted fans,
And proudly springing beauteous crest
Of shoots all brown with glistening down,
Curved like the lyre-bird's tail half spread,
Or necks opposed of wrangling swans,
Red bill to bill, black breast to breast, —
Ay! in this realm of seeming rest,

What sights you met and sounds of dread!
Calcareous caldrons, deep and large
With geysers hissing to their marge;
Sulphureous fumes that spout and blow;
Columns and cones of boiling snow;
And sable lazy-bubbling pools
Of sputtering mud that never cools;
With jets of steam through narrow vents
Uproaring, maddening to the sky,
Like cannon-mouths that shoot on high,
In unremitting loud discharge,
Their inexhaustible contents;
While oft beneath the trembling ground
Rumbles a drear persistent sound
Like ponderous engines infinite, working
At some tremendous task below!
Such are the signs and symptoms — lurking
Or launching forth in dread display —
Of hidden fires, internal strife,
Amid that leafy, lush array
Of rank luxuriant verdurous life:
Glad haunts above where blissful love
Might revel, rove, enraptured dwell;
But through them pierce such tokens fierce
Of rage beneath and frenzies fell;
As if, to quench and stille it,
Green Paradise were flung o'er Hell, —
Flung fresh with all her bowers close-knit,
Her dewy vales and dimpled streams;
Yet could not so its fury quell
But that the old red realm accurst

Would still recalcitrate, rebel,
Still struggle upward and outburst
In scalding fumes, sulphureous steams.
It struck you as you paused to trace
The sunny scenery's strange extremes,
As if in some divinest face,
All heavenly smiles, divinest grace,
Your eye at times discerned, despite
Sweet looks with innocence elate,
Some wan, wild spasm of blank affright,
Or demon scowl of pent-up hate;
Or some convulsive writhe confest,
For all that bloom of beauty bright,
An anguish not to be represt.
You look, — a moment bask in, bless,
Its laughing light of happiness;
But look again, — what startling throes
And fiery pangs of fierce distress   ·
The lovely lineaments disclose, —
How o'er the fascinating features flit
The genuine passions of the nether pit!

Alfred Domett.

FOREST AND SEA-SHORE.

AND thus o'er many a mountain wood-entangled,
    And stony plain of stunted fern that hides
The bright-green oily anise; and hillsides
And valleys, where its dense luxuriance balks
With interclinging fronds and tough red stalks
The traveller's hard-fought path, they took their way.

Sometimes they traversed, half the dreary day,
A deep-glenned wilderness all dark and dank
With trees, whence tattered and dishevelled dangled
Pale streaming strips of mosses long and lank;
Where at each second step of tedious toil
On perfect forms of fallen trunks they tread,
And ankle-deep sink in their yielding bed, —
Moss-covered rottenness long turned to soil, —
Until, ascending ever in the drear
Dumb gloom forlorn, a sudden rushing sound
Of pattering rain strikes freshly on the ear, —
'T is but the breeze that up so high has found
Amid the rattling leaves a free career!
To the soft, mighty, sea-like roar they list:
Or else 't is calm; the gloom itself is gone;
And all is airiness and light-filled mist,
As on the open mountain-side, so lone
And lofty, freely breathing they emerge.
And sometimes through a league-long swamp they urge
Slow progress, dragging through foot-sucking slush
Their weary limbs, red-painted to the knees
In pap rust-stained by iron or seeding rush;
But soon through limpid brilliant streams that travel
With murmuring, momentary-gleaming foam
That flits and flashes over sun-warmed gravel
They wade, and laughing wash that unctuous loam
Off blood-stained limbs now clean beyond all cavil
And start refreshed new road-knots to unravel.
And what delight, at length, that glimpse instils,
That wedge-shaped opening in the wooded hills,
Which, like a cup, the far-off ocean fills!

Anon they skirt the winding wild sea-shore;
From woody crag or ferny bluff admiring
The dim-bright beautiful blue bloom it wore,
That still Immensity, that placid Ocean,
With all its thousand leagues of level calm,
Tremendously serene; he, fancying more
Than feeling, for tired spirits peace-desiring,
With the world-fret and life's low fever sore,
Weary and worn with turmoil and emotion,
The soothing might of its majestic balm.
Or to the beach descending, with joined hands
They pace the firm tide-saturated sands
Whitening beneath their footpress as they pass;
And from that fresh and tender marble floor
So glossy-shining in the morning sun,
Watch the broad billows at their chase untiring, —
How they come rolling on, in rougher weather, —
How in long lines they swell and link together,
Till, as their watery walls they grandly lift,
Their level crests extending sideways, swift
Shoot over into headlong roofs of glass
Cylindric, thundering as they curl and run
And close, down-rushing to a weltering dance
Of foam that slides along the smooth expanse,
Nor seldom, in a streaked and creamy sheet
Comes unexpected hissing round their feet,
While with great leaps and hurry-skurry fleet,
His louder laughter mixed with hers so sweet,
Each tries to stop the other's quick retreat.
Or else on sands that, white and loose, give way
At every step, they toil, till labor-sped

Their limbs in the noon-loneliness they lay
On that hot, soft, yet unelastic bed,
With brittle seaweed, pink and black, o'erstrewn,
And wrecks of many a forest-growth upthrown,
Bare stem and barkless branches, clean, sea-bleached,
Milk-white, or stringy logs deep-red as wine,
Their ends ground smooth against a thousand rocks,
Dead-heavy, soaked with penetrating brine;
Or bolted fragment of some ship storm-breached
And shattered, — all with barnacles o'ergrown,
Gray-crusted thick with hollow-coned small shells, —
So silent in the sunshine still and lone,
So reticent of what it sadly tells.

Alfred Domett.

SILENT CATARACTS.

FROM the low sky-line of the hilly range
   Before them, sweeping down its dark-green face
Into the lake that slumbered at its base,
A mighty cataract, so it seemed,
Over a hundred steps of marble streamed
And gushed, or fell in dripping overflow. —
Flat steps, in flights half-circled, — row o'er row,
Irregularly mingling side by side;
They and the torrent-curtain wide,
All rosy-hued, it seemed, with sunset's glow. —
But what is this! no roar, no sound,
Disturbs that torrent's hush profound!
The wanderers near and nearer come, —
Still is the mighty cataract dumb!

A thousand fairy lights may shimmer
With tender sheen, with glossy glimmer,
O'er curve advanced and salient edge
Of many a luminous water-ledge;
A thousand slanting shadows pale
May fling their thin transparent veil
O'er deep recess and shallow dent
In many a watery stair's descent:
Yet, mellow-bright, or mildly dim,
Both lights and shades, both dent and rim,
Each wavy streak, each warm snow-tress,
Stand rigid, mute, and motionless!
No faintest murmur, not a sound,
Relieves that cataract's hush profound;
No tiniest bubble, not a flake
Of floating foam, is seen to break
The smoothness where it meets the lake;
Along that shining surface move
No ripples; not the slightest swell
Rolls o'er the mirror darkly green,
Where, every feature limned so well,
Pale, silent, and serene as death,
The cataract's image hangs beneath
The cataract, but not more serene,
More phantom-silent, than is seen
The white rose-hued reality above.

They paddle past, for on the right
Another cataract comes in sight;
Another broader, grander flight
Of steps, all stainless, snowy-bright!

They land, — their curious way they track
Near thickets made by contrast black;
And then that wonder seems to be
A cataract carved in Parian stone,
Or any purer substance known, —
Agate or milk-chalcedony!
Its showering snow-cascades appear
Long ranges bright of stalactite,
And sparry frets and fringes white,
Thick-falling, plenteous, tier o'er tier;
Its crowding stairs, in bold ascent
Piled up that silvery-glimmering height,
Are layers, they know, accretions slow
Of hard silicious sediment:
For as they gain a rugged road,
And cautious climb the solid rime,
Each step becomes a terrace broad,
Each terrace a wide basin brimmed
With water, brilliant, yet in hue
The tenderest, delicate harebell-blue
Deepening to violet! Slowly climb
The twain, and turn from time to time
To mark the hundred baths in view, —
Crystalline azure, snowy-rimmed, –
The marge of every beauteous pond
Curve after curve, each lower beyond
The higher, outsweeping white and wide,
Like snowy lines of foam that glide
O'er level sea-sands lightly skimmed
By thin sheets of the glistening tide.
They climb those milk-white flats incrusted

And netted o'er with wavy ropes
Of wrinkled silica. At last,
Each basin's heat increasing fast,
The topmost step the pair surmount,
And lo, the cause of all! Around,
The circling cliffs a crater bound, —
Cliffs damp with dark-green moss, their slopes
All crimson-stained with blots and streaks,
White-mottled and vermilion-rusted;
And in the midst, beneath a cloud
That ever upward rolls and reeks
And hides the sky with its dim shroud,
Look where upshoots a fuming fount, —
Up through a blue and boiling pool
Perennial, — a great sapphire steaming,
In that coralline crater gleaming.
Upwelling ever, amethystal,
Ebullient comes the bubbling crystal!
Still growing cooler and more cool
As down the porcelain stairway slips
The fluid flint, and slowly drips,
And hangs each basin's curling lips
With crusted fringe each year increases,
Thicker than shear-forgotten fleeces;
More close and regular than rows,
Long rows of snowy trumpet-flowers
Some day to hang in garden-bowers,
When strangers shall these wilds enclose.

Alfred Domett.

Sandwich Islands.

KILAUEA.

DEEP Hades of the seven Phlegethons!
From thy basaltic pillared walls I gaze,
Through sulphurous clouds that ceaselessly ascend
From fiery maelstroms in red, rushing whirl,
Into thy vast abyss with silent awe.

Eve's curtains gather round thee like a shroud,
And drape in shadow Mauna Loa's dome;
The trade-wind o'er the bending forest sweeps,
Cold and mist-laden from the eastern wave;
And as it parts the fire-born clouds below,
The smouldering ruins of a city vast —
A giant Moscow in a sea of flame —
Appear with blackened walls, and dome and spire
Of church and grand cathedral crashing fall;
Turret and tower and monument go down,
As round them lap and whirl the eddying flames,
Like those lost cities which Jehovah's wrath
O'erwhelmed in sulphury hail and fiery rain,
Till from the ruined plain the smoke went up,
Seething and dense as from a furnace blast.

       *   *   *

   Thou fiery wonder of the untaught mind!
The simple natives of the isles had made
A home in thee for Pele, — fiery power,
Goddess of the volcano's hot domain;
How like the ancient Greeks, who wove their dreams

Of the ideal in poetic forms,
And robed Cocytus' son with Pele's power
Over their burning, weird, infernal river.

No Stygian waves surround thy Hades deep,
No Iris bright descends with golden vase,
To bring the dreaded draught to perjured gods;
Yet thy wild, fiery glare hath lighted up
A scene more brilliant than Greek poet's dream,
Sublime in moral courage and the faith
That rent asunder superstition's chains,
And by her incandescent throne of power,
Defied the Goddess Pele in thy depths.

Kapiolani -- noblest of her race, --
Kapiolani — type of womankind, --
In high moral heroism born of love,
In past or present and in every clime,
Immortal as the faith which fired her heart,
Her deed sheds lustre on these ocean isles!

       *   *   *

O'er fire-browned clinkers and through tangled woods,
Up mountain steeps a hundred miles she walked,
Trampling the creeds of ages 'neath her feet,
Braving the wrath of all the mythic gods,
That, like dark incubi on heart and brain,
Had checked the progress of Hawaii's race,
She sought thy depths to tempt and to defy
The rage, the power of their multiple gods;
While awe-struck thousands on thy lofty rim
Gazed tremblingly beneath in firm belief
That Pele in her wrath would hurl her fires
On one who dared her in her sulphury home.

Her brow all radiantly illumed by hope,
She stood beside thy rushing, liquid tide
Of red-hot lava in its maddest flow,
And as the sulphury vapors, wreathing, rolled
In eddying fire-lit waves round her tall form,
She seemed divine as thus she calmly spoke:
"In His great name who died for men I come,
To prove to my lost race the living God!
And here, O Pele! superstition's myth!
I do defy thee on thy throne of power!
If thou existest, whelm me 'neath thy waves,
Pour on me all thy scorching lava flood,
Or suffocate me with thy sulphury breath,
Or close around me all thy lakes of fire!
But no,—the fresh breeze lifts the sulphury clouds,
The waves subside, the fiery jets decrease;
God calms thy vortex as the restless sea;
I trample here on thy pretended power,
And cry, Io Jehova! in thy depths;
Io Jehova! let the triumph ring,
Till all the isles shall know the living God!"
She passed majestic o'er the lava vale,
As a triumphant smile illumed her face,
God-like and noble, born of faith and hope.
Now sable night hangs o'er thee, Kilauea,
But night illumined by thy sulphury glare;
Thy seven seething lakes light up the clouds
With an unearthly and demoniac glow,
The fever flush from thy hot heart of flame,
The hectic glow of an expiring world.

*   *   *

Now the waves flash, and, eddying, whirl and leap
'Gainst crumbling shores of glass-like lava cliffs,
Where Pele's fair hair waves in sulphury steam;
The fiery jets, fierce bubbling, chase each other,
Like flame-maned coursers on their burning track,
Then disappear, lost in the raging gulf;
Ever with northward flow the current sweeps,
Crackling and sparkling in red fissures deep,
As the cooled surface breaks, like fields of ice,
And dark-red lava heaps in fiery drift.

          *   *   *

Thou seemest not of earth; thy red waves come,
Up, — rushing from that central, fiery sea,
Beneath earth's ocean that resistless wars
With all that forms this planet's fragile crust.
And as I gaze upon thy deep abyss,
Thoughts of the grandeur of Eternal Power
Sweep o'er the mind in wild magnificence,
To far past ages, when Creative Will
Flashed through this planet's incandescent mass
Ere the earth's crust was cooled, or the vast sea,
Condensing, fell from seething atmosphere,
On lava beds just cooling round the poles.
Around me are God's forges, in the domes
Of mountains vast that pierce the blue of heaven,
And from their snowy diadems look down
On plains of lava blackening to the sea,
And in the line of lessening cones that sweep
From thy weird chasm by pit-craters deep;
Here in Time's morn, red columns flamed from ocean,
Hurled boiling back the hot and vapory waves,

With blazing cataracts of liquid fire,
Till this great isle arose, a smoking mass
Of fire-scorched cinders, as the giant tread
Of the mad earthquake stamped it into form!

*   *   *

W. C. Jones.

LAHAINA.

WHERE the wave tumbles;
  Where the reef rumbles;
Where the sea sweeps
  Under bending palm-branches,
Sliding its snow-white
  And swift avalanches;
Where the sails pass
O'er an ocean of glass,
  Or trail their dull anchors
Down in the sea-grass.

Where the hills smoulder;
  Where the plains smoke;
Where the peaks shoulder
  The clouds like a yoke;
Where the dear isle
Has a charm to beguile
  As she rests in the lap
Of the seas that enfold her.

Where shadows falter;
  Where the mist hovers
  Like steam that covers
Some ancient altar.

Where the sky rests
On deep wooded crests;
  Where the clouds lag, —
Where the sun floats
His glittering moats,
Swimming the rainbows
  That girdle the crag.

Where the new-comer
In deathless summer
  Dreams away troubles;
Where the grape blossoms
And blows its sweet bubbles.

Where the goats cry
  From the hillside corral;
Where the fish leap
  In the weedy canal, —
In the shallow lagoon
  With its waters forsaken, —
Where the dawn struggles
  With night for an hour,
Then breaks like a tropical
  Bird from its bower.

Where from the long leaves
  The fresh dew is shaken;
Where the wind sleeps
  And where the birds waken !
                    Charles Warren Stoddard.

KAMEHAMEHA HYMN.

HAWAII! sea-girt land!
  Strong for thy monarch stand;
Sons of the ancient band,
    Stand for your King!

Hawaii's true-born sons,
Cherish the high-born ones, —
From old their lineage runs,
    Guard the young chiefs!

Hawaii! young and brave,
Thine 't is thyself to save!
Hopeful thy banner wave —
    Upward, and on!

O Thou who reign'st above,
Father of might and love!
Grant that thy peaceful dove
    Brood o'er our land.
          King Kalakaua. Tr. H. L. Sheldon.

HAWAIIAN NATIONAL ANTHEM.

ETERNAL Father, mighty God!
  Behold us, from thy blest abode;
To thee we turn, for thou wilt care
To listen to our humble prayer.

May gentle peace forever reign
O'er these fair islands of the main,
Hawaii's peaks to Niihau's strand,
The peace of God o'er all the land!
   Forever be our country free,
   Our laws and Heaven's in harmony.
   All hearts respond, all voices sing,
   God save, God save our gracious King!

And may our Chieftains ever be,
Guided, O Lord, by love to Thee,
And all the people join to raise
One universal song of praise.
God save the people of our land,
Uphold by thine Almighty hand;
Thy watchful care defends from harm,
Faithful and sure thy sovereign arm.
   Forever be our country free,
   Our laws and Heaven's in harmony,
   All hearts respond, all voices sing,
   God save, God save our gracious King.
                Lilia K. Dominis.   Tr. H. L. Sheldon.

THE BEACH AT HILO BAY.

WHAT has this grand, curved beach to show?
   Slimy wharves, in the sun aglow?
Warehouses grim, in a dismal row,
Stretching for weary miles? No, no!

Gracefully fringed it is, with trees
Nodding obeisance to every breeze
Born on the mountain or on the high seas.

Under the trees the lagoons are asleep,
Children dumb of the roaring deep,
Into their cradle the wild waves peep.

Darling gem is each bright lagoon,
Molten silver at fervid noon,
Burnished mirror for evening's moon.

Birds on the smooth, packed sand are parading,
Legs stripped bare, all ready for wading,
Or daintily poised, the foam-crest evading.

Here is the tablet the waves prepare
For ragged school artists, so burnt and bare,
With faces begrimmed, and tangled hair.

And on this easel so smoothly sanded
Fleets are sketched by the deftly handed, —
You would think the Royal Navy was stranded.

Queer little crabs are making their tracks,
With dinners robbed from their neighbors' sacks,
And stolen houses upon their backs.

Here are mosses in rarest green
And royal purple, fit for a queen,
Which painters may envy in vain, I ween.

And blue-eyed flowers, with faces bland,
All untended by human hand,
Asking nothing but sunshine and sand.

Yonder are snow-tipped mountains bold,
Always new, though a cycle old,
Full of fire as their sides can hold.

Nearer at hand, — no tongue can tell,
The mighty magic of beauty's spell,
That wakes our smiles, and tears as well.

Rarest beauties our beach can show,
As bounding along its crescent we go,
Or lost in thought we saunter slow, —
And the half has not yet been told, — no, no!

                                        F. Coan.

EPILOGUE.

TRAVELS AT HOME.

OFT have I wished a traveller to be:
  Mine eyes did even itch the sights to see,
That I had heard and read of. Oft I have
Been greedy of occasion, as the grave,
That never says enough; yet still was crost,
When opportunities had promised most.
At last I said, what mean'st thou, wandering elf,
To straggle thus? Go travel first thyself.
Thy little world can show thee wonders great:
The greater may have more, but not more neat
And curious pieces. Search, and thou shalt find
Enough to talk of. If thou wilt, thy mind
Europe supplies, and Asia thy will,
And Afric thine affections. And if still
Thou list to travel further, put thy senses
For both the Indies. Make no more pretences
Of new discoveries, whilst yet thine own,
And nearest, little world is still unknown.
Away then with thy quadrants, compasses,
Globes, tables, cards, and maps, and minute glasses:
Lay by thy journals and thy diaries,

Close up thine annals and thine histories.
Study thyself, and read what thou hast writ
In thine own book, thy conscience. Is it fit
To labor after other knowledge so,
And thine own nearest, dearest self not know?
Travels abroad both dear and dangerous are,
Whilst oft the soul pays for the body's fare:
Travels at home are cheap, and safe. Salvation
Comes mounted on the wings of meditation.
He that doth live at home, and learns to know
God and himself, needeth no further go.

George Herbert.

HOME.

THERE is a land, of every land the pride,
Beloved by Heaven o'er all the world beside;
Where brighter suns dispense serener light,
And milder moons emparadise the night;
A land of beauty, virtue, valor, truth,
Time-tutored age, and love-exalted youth;
The wandering mariner, whose eye explores
The wealthiest isles, the most enchanting shores,
Views not a realm so bountiful and fair,
Nor breathes the spirit of a purer air;
In every clime the magnet of his soul,
Touched by remembrance, trembles to that pole;
For in this land of Heaven's peculiar grace,
The heritage of nature's noblest race,
There is a spot of earth supremely blest,

A dearer, sweeter spot than all the rest,
Where man, creation's tyrant, casts aside
His sword and sceptre, pageantry and pride,
While in his softened looks benignly blend
The sire, the son, the husband, brother, friend :
Here woman reigns; the mother, daughter, wife,
Strews with fresh flowers the narrow way of life ;
In the clear heaven of her delightful eye,
An angel-guard of loves and graces lie ;
Around her knees domestic duties meet,
And fireside pleasures gambol at her feet.
"Where shall that land, that spot of earth, be found?"
Art thou a man? — a patriot? — look around ;
Oh, thou shalt find, howe'er thy footsteps roam,
That land thy country, and that spot thy home !

On Greenland's rocks, o'er rude Kamschatka's plains,
In pale Siberia's desolate domains ;
Where the wild hunter takes his lonely way,
Tracks through tempestuous snows his savage prey,
The reindeer's spoil, the ermine's treasure, shares,
And feasts his famine on the fat of bears ;
Or, wrestling with the might of raging seas,
Where round the pole the eternal billows freeze,
Plucks from their jaws the stricken whale, in vain
Plunging down headlong through the whirling main ;
His wastes of ice are lovelier in his eye
Than all the flowery vales beneath the sky ;
And dearer far than Cæsar's palace-dome,
His cavern-shelter, and his cottage-home.

O'er China's garden-fields and peopled floods;
In California's pathless world of woods;
Round Andes' heights, where Winter, from his throne,
Looks down in scorn upon the Summer zone;
By the gay borders of Bermuda's isles,
Where Spring with everlasting verdure smiles;
On pure Madeira's vine-robed hills of health;
In Java's swamps of pestilence and wealth;
Where Babel stood, where wolves and jackals drink,
Midst weeping willows, on Euphrates' brink;
On Carmel's crest; by Jordan's reverend stream,
Where Canaan's glories vanished like a dream;
Where Greece, a spectre, haunts her heroes' graves,
And Rome's vast ruins darken Tiber's waves;
Where broken-hearted Switzerland bewails
Her subject mountains and dishonored vales;
Where Albion's rocks exult amidst the sea,
Around the beauteous isle of Liberty;
Man, through all ages of revolving time,
Unchanging man, in every varying clime,
Deems his own land of every land the pride,
Beloved by Heaven o'er all the world beside;
His home the spot of earth supremely blest,
A dearer, sweeter spot than all the rest.

James Montgomery.

THE END.

Electrotyped and Printed at the University Press, Cambridge.